When Bindiya Rebelled

Vaneeta Vaid

KNOWLEDGE WORLD

KW Publishers Pvt Ltd
New Delhi

KNOWLEDGE WORLD

KW Publishers Pvt Ltd

4676/21, First Floor, Ansari Road, Daryaganj, New Delhi 110002

E knowledgeworld@vsnl.net **T** +91.11.23263498 / 43528107

w w w . k w p u b . c o m

ISBN 978-93-80502-93-9

One

Twelve-year-old Bindiya stuck the 'neem daatun', (twig broken off a neem tree), into her mouth and thought of nothing but scraping the 'cow dung,' (gobar), with her bare hands from the dusty path. She dropped it into Shanta, her mother's, basket. Shanta, held the basket over her head and obligingly tilted it, as Bindiya stretched on her toes to deposit cattle waste into the bottom of the roughly woven bamboo basket. For Bindiya or her family, cow dung was precious and not unclean. It was fuel for lighting their cooking stoves or 'chula's'. 'Pstoooooo' Bindiya spat out the threads of the 'neem stick,' or daatun, she was chewing. Even Shanta chewed a stick as she walked. This was how they brushed their teeth!

Soon the bitter juices from the sticks cleansed their mouths and they threw them away.

After a little while Bindiya spotted some cows grazing. The mother and daughter duo waited and soon were rewarded with more dung. Bindiya scooped up some mud and dry 'washed' her hands with the mud; rubbing off so the mud fell off in small rolls to the ground.

Even though they had awoken very early much before dawn, already the village ladies were up and about. Their husbands were 'tillers,' labour that cultivates or tills land, of the farm lands. They did not own any land or cattle, but were in fact custodians of the existing land/cattle for the landlord of this area.

Shanta and Bindiya crossed over to the middle of a field, where a neighbour named Sunheri, also Bindiya's best friend Jhumri's mother, along with some other ladies was making piles of already prepared, hard, dried dung cakes.

How are you?" Shanta smiled a greeting before squatting besides them and joining them in what they were doing. But before all that, Shanta, kneaded her left ankle to ease the stinging pain that had started up. She had permanent pain in her ankle, as a result of an accident. Sunheri looked at her sympathetically then shifted, so Shanta could share the space more comfortably. Shanta checked the dung cake to make sure it was completely dry, before she passed it on to one of the ladies making the pile.

Hay piles were a common sight in these areas. They were actually storage of dung cakes! First the cakes would be balanced to stand in a pyramid mode. Then the cakes would be covered/ layered by hay or fresh dung and tied. This was to ensure protection from rain. The layering was done with a technique to form waist high piles! Such heaps of hay/dung dotted the fields at distances! Each member of the village took cakes freely from here when needed on the condition that hay/dung piles continued to be made as replacement! This ensured an unending supply of 'dung,' fuel for their stoves!

Not joining them, Bindiya pulled at a straw and ran after the herd of goats grazing in the fi elds. She lifted up a protesting lamb and rocked it as one would a baby. Digging her feet deep into the wet mud, Bindiya chortled loving the squishy feeling. The lamb 'baaaed', this made Bindiya laugh out aloud. She began to baby talk to the lamb simultaneously rocking it like a baby. Her mother shook her head hiding a smile. She muttered to Sunheri, "what a baby she herself is ....!"

The lamb bleated and struggled to jump off and Bindiya scolded it saying, "don't be naughty…Maalik, the landlord, owns all this land and he will banish you if you don't behave!"

Bindiya was just repeating sentences that she often heard.

"You are lucky the wound of your ankle healed."

"Why would it not? My ankle was wounded years ago….Dayaji, the village medicine man, cured me!" Shanta grunted, still on her haunches dispensing dung cakes to another lady.

"I know Shanta. Only thing is, do you know Bholu (a tiller) died last night." Sunheri said in a low voice.

"Really…his wound did not heal?"

"No, fever increased and it festered, the wound I mean, Dayaji, even washed it with cow urine…poultice….but he succumbed……" Bindiya heard this conversation in the background, but was not really paying much attention since she was having so much fun running after the goats.

Some time passed and work continued.

"Enough for the day; let us return home," Shanta finally said to Sunheri; likewise the group began to disperse. With satisfaction the ladies viewed their handiwork before bidding farewell to each other. Bindiya also saw that hay stacks had been mounded, "time to go!" Putting the Lamb down, Bindiya scuttled after her mother, who was stepping down the paths with a rhythmic walk. The common dress for ladies in these parts was the 'sari', (long unstitched, five meters- plus, of cloth). They covered their heads with the long flowing part of their sari and their 'sari veil' did not slip even on the hottest of days! Growing girls wore salwar, kameez suits, long shirt-loose pyjamas.

Men folk wore 'pant-shirt' mostly. Some older men still wore the traditional 'dhoti,' (yards of untitched cloth), with 'kurta's,' long shirt, however. Thick rubber sandals were worn by men and women both. And children like Bindiya wore frocks for girls and shorts and shirt for boys.

Dawn had completely broken by now. They crossed more ploughed fields, till they neared their very small settlement. The 'chuk- chuk' of the tube wells and groan of the plough tractor broke the air. Shanta and Bindiya joined other neighbouring ladies walking home. Their voices rose like a cloud of sing song tones, synchronizing into the atmosphere naturally; as they negotiated the muddy paths between the fields, with baskets over their heads.

Spring was slowly giving way to summers. Good rains had certified a very good harvest! A general sense of well being had permeated the atmosphere! The cycle of seasons ensured no one in this vicinity, at least, was idle. These were people of the soil; the constant battle in adjusting with nature's ups and downs made this populace hard working! Be it winters, spring, summer or fall they had to coordinate day to day living with the climate in order to survive. The geographical dimensions of these lands saw widely spread out small tiller settlements, or tiny villages, skirting the farm lands. Bindiya's village was one such settlement. Unstructured habitation, caused maybe by the proximity to a pond or well, decided the beginning of a settlement!

Constructing of huts was done by the tiller's themselves! No blue prints of house plans, builders or architects were required here! They made their own huts, drains, and living spaces! This showed up in the architecture though. Some huts were made in a certain way to fullfill the requirement of that particular family living there—other huts built some other way. A wall here or pillar there even though it did not look good emerged with passing time and requirements; leading to a very non-uniformity resident lane!

The tillers and their families worked hard to survive. They possessed nothing of their own except their huts and an intense loyalty to the landlord who employed them to work.

As a matter of fact, apart from possessing extensive land hereabouts, the landlord owned a large mix of goats, cows, and buffaloes too. The tiller/villagers were also allowed to distribute milk from two milch cows amongst themselves and the rest of the milk went to the landlord.

Shri Girdhari, the landlord had studied in the city and then had gone abroad for a very long time. When his father grew old, Shri Girdhari or the 'Maalik,' (boss) as he was referred to, returned to take charge of his properties and innovate on how to administer their large holdings so he could get the best monetary benefits! Unfortunately Shri Girdhari never visited his tenants /tillers. All his employees went to him, at the 'Haveli' (Mansion).

They in turn *never invited* him to the village willingly. *They also never complained about anything*! He was like God for them moreover they tried their best not to come to his notice all the time. How they settled to work with him, or their welfare was expected not to be of his concern! It was handled by the chain of employed help!

"It is better for us to remain at a distance! You never know when we say something wrong and get into trouble", Deven, Bindiya's father, would always caution if the 'invisible' landlord was ever discussed!

This began a pattern of behaviour that saw 'Maalik's' non presence since no one ever complained about anything along with the tillers rigorous adjustments and accommodating mind-set. Leading to a dreading fear that if ever anyone carried woes to Maalik he or she was breaching some unsaid pact!

"Tum, tum, tum, tum!" Bindiya hummed an old folk song as she skipped on her way.

Bindiya, taking advantage of her slight built squeezed in through two very heavy and wildly growing bushes that made natural hedges along the 'kutcha,' (unpaved, trails). Her mother and the other ladies had to go around this hedging to reach to the other side! They smiled when Bindiya met them on the other side, grinning from ear to ear. Bindiya was physically quite under developed for her age. She was slender and small and was easily mistaken to be much younger then she actually was.

Hours out in the sun had polished her skin to burnished gold along with her hair that too was sun bleached! Two saucer-shaped brown eyes joined a button nose and wide smiling mouth on a round face!

Bindiya pranced forward, measuring a good distance between the group and herself before she had to stop.

"Ufff" Bindiya's worn rubber slippers stuck into a patch of slushy mud. "Please don't break" she addressed the worn out slippers as she gently pulled them out of the swampy mud patch, "there is still time for Ma and Bapu to go to the 'haat,' (market), and buy me a new pair!"

"AAAAH" triumphantly Bindiya managed to pull out the slippers without damage! Regardless that the slippers were covered with earth, Bindiya slipped them on. Wet mud coated and cooled her heels and ankles. Rubbing her feet on the back of her leg, Bindiya tried her best to clean up! Giving up she sashayed down the grassy paths still humming under her breath.

With a squeal she stopped by the blue berry, (Jamun), tree. Bindiya could not wait for the rains to come. Fat heavy drops would sink into the heat dried grounds carving rivulets into the hard surface. Quenching their thirsts the tree would preen with 'Jamun's,' (blue berry), that to Bindiya's mind resembled a Queen's ornaments! She and her friends would scoop up handfuls and suck the berries, comparing their blue-stained tongues merrily; YES! Bindiya could hardly wait! But the rains were at least three months away!

Hopping and pirouetting like a ballerina, Bindiya further down encircled the mango orchard. Her eyes caught an easily accessible raw mango just above her head. "I can effortlessly stone this one!" Bindiya thought.

Immobile for ten seconds, Bindiya checked to see if anyone was looking. No one was! Her mother, busy chatting with her friends, had moved ahead. There was no one else around. Picking up a stone and with one accurate flick, 'thwack' Bindiya managed to shoot down the small raw of mango! The raw mango rolled down to her feet. "You are mine!" Bindiya ominously crunched in a mock threat, picking up her loot! Wiping her trophy with her the hem of her frock, Bindiya bit the raw mango; her taste buds savouring the sour tang of the fruit. It was mango season now. The landlord owned all the fruit orchards. Two weeks more and the mangoes would be plucked and packaged and sold in the 'mandi,' bazaar.

Actually times had changed. Big corporate houses had already purchased all the mangoes. Earlier the farmers, in this case Shri Girdhari, directly sold their produce in the market. Now these corporate houses purchased the crop/fruit from the source that is the orchards or farms and marketed it themselves.

The representatives of these business houses came in trucks; with huge packaging crates and picked up the ware! There would be general pandemonium when all that started!

Bindiya, her brothers and friends usually escaped from their chores and waited around here, hoping to smuggle mangoes to eat when the supervisors were not looking!

Bindiya caught up with her mother; throwing the finished mango kernel into the drain when she reached home. The second house to the left in the lane was theirs. Their village was made up of five houses. These houses haphazardly made up a stretch or lane. If you entered the lane you met a muddy path flanked by an open drain that ran along the right side till the lane ended.

There were four such small villages where tillers from Shri Girdhari's farms had made their dwellings. Each village was at some distance from each other though!

Outside the resident area was a banyan tree encircled by a cemented platform, which was an open 'town hall' of some sorts. The men-folk sat and 'discussed' things over there collectively!

As of now, the six elderly gentlemen of the village, as well as from a neighbouring village, sat and played cards under the shady tree. The cards were faded pack, but very prized!

A small circle of men, also sat away from them sucking from smoke from a 'hookah,' hubble bubble. They sketched a content and languid picture, so typical of rural equanimity, calmness! Bindiya skipped past two goats, a donkey, and some dogs also sharing the repose with the men folk!

"Greeting!" The card group members toothlessly smiled, when Bindiya hailed them with a greeting.

The rest of the area was farm lands. As mentioned before these farmlands were owned by Sri Girdhariji. He had employed Bindiya's father and the other men of the village as tillers. He paid them monthly wages.

Bindiya had never been to the 'Haveli' but she knew after the cattle sheds came the 'bada road,' (high way), and that led them to the Mansion. Her village was tucked away and considered to be a little within the interior as compared to the other villages.

"OOOOOOOOOOOOO!" Bindiya teased two stray dogs only to bump into an errant hen clucking past!

Outside one house stood a donkey. The donkey later in day would pull a cart of hay. Similarly at a distance two buffaloes were tied to keg. A pile of fodder that they chewed thoughtfully denoted it was their breakfast time! They would be taken to the fields later in the day.

At Bindiya's hut entrance, was parked a decaying hand-pulled cart. Deven usually was promising himself that he would attach a cycle to the cart for better comfort. He really never got down to fulfilling this promise!

"Watch it!" Kanta 'Bhabhi,' (term of respect), cautioned, as she led two buffaloes out of the lane. Grinning Bindiya pressed back as the black bovines trudged forward.

"*Bindiya didi*, (sister), Bindiya didi lets play!" shouted a group of village urchins. They were playing 'Pitoo.' This game was about making a tower with seven flat stones and hitting it with a ball. These children did not have a ball, so they used a slightly larger and rounder stone, to target the tower!

"No, no, Ma needs me…later maybe!" Bindiya refused in a bright voice, not stopping in her stride.

Bindiya's village comprised of sun-bleached, cakes huts. These huts were usually constructed from mud blocks. The roofs were thatched or made of mud tiles and the floors covered with a mud and cow-dung paste, which supposedly served as a disinfectant. A semi circle low wall fenced each hut. The front of the hut was introduced by an outer courtyard. Sacks of wheat were stacked in the corners here. Another opening led to the inner sanctum. This was again a courtyard edged by two rooms facing the entrances.

One room was full of hay, coal, wood, and farm implements. It was called the 'kotari' or store room; the other was the sleeping quarters; where Bindiya, her two brothers and parents slept. On the wall facing the entry was adorned a big poster of the monkey God Hanuman. Shanta now and then invoked the blessings of the almighty by chanting out 'bhajans,' hymn, in front of the poster. Nature and its entities was the subject of their prayers. Prayers for good rains, good crop, and no drought led them through their lives! Once in a while the entire family left early and visited the village temple, which was forty-five minutes walk from where they were. This was considered to be an exciting excursion for the kids!

When hot winds blew in during summers the family slept outside under the stars in the outer court yard. As of now since the weather was fine, they slept inside.

In this room was one rope bed. It was for Bindiya's father. Bindiya, her two brothers, and mother spread mats and slept on the floor. Their father was the strength of the family. All privileges were his. He was served food first, his decisions were ultimate.

His interaction with all of them was circumspect. He was the bread winner and had to be treated thus. Though the 'bed room' had no door, the 'kotari' had an unpolished, heavy door; whittled out of wood from tree trunks by Bindiya's father! This door was not attached on hinges! *It was not attached at all!*

In fact it independently was parked by the side of the 'kotari!' At night this makeshift door was lifted and used to cover the entrance of the 'kotari!' This was done for some vague security measure. That the door was taller than the entrance mattered not.

"YERGHHHHHHH!" Bindiya thumbed a nose at the strays, lazing right inside the entrance. One stray growled and shot towards her.

"Waaaaahhhhhh!" Bindiya giggling helplessly dashed and almost bumped into the home- made air cooler, reposed at the side!

One ingenious apparatus was the home made 'cooler.' Bindiya's father went to the city once and he picked up a table fan. During summers the table fan was placed on an over turned drum. In front of the fan was placed standing a rope 'charpoy,' bed. The 'charpoy' was soaked with water and its surface weaved, poked, and parted at sporadic intervals to allow air to waft through! At night, when the summer heat prevailed unbearably, the family slept outdoors. The cooler was then activated; the fan was switched on, by jamming two wires, so a breeze blew into the dampened rope bed transmitting cool air; thus providing relief from the blistering heat! Now and then someone would soak the 'charpoy' to keep it continuously wet!

Every house in the area followed suit and created their rope bed coolers too! During summers, it was not surprising to see wires snaking up the pole, changing the landscaping! Long, long naked wire connecting the electric pole, meshed a criss-cross of wires over head!

Bindiya's village had electricity, but it was as good as having none! The electricity was mostly off! The light bulbs in the hut were dirty and grimy and had lost their use a long time ago. They had a singular electric pole, stationed at the lane entry. This 'street' light had been installed years ago. It provided regular 'light.' Hooking on to the pole and 'stealing' light was a harmless crime considered as simple as a white lie!

However two incidents should have deterred the dwellers of this lane from poaching electricity. One, a short circuit had caused a major fire last year. Luckily no one died. But two houses nearer to the pole bore the brunt of the fire and their blackened walls still showed evidence!! Two, Leela 'Bhabhi' had been electrocuted and saved by providence, when she stepped on a live wire, detached from the pole during a storm. The villagers never asked for help. Pappu, one of the inhabitants, who prided himself on knowledge about electric fittings re-attached the wire at a very high risk to his own person! As far as a fire was concerned, "could happen anywhere!" shrugged one and all.

Since Leela 'Bhabhi' had survived everything was good! So they continued to live in this fire hazard, high risk situation till the next disaster!

Presently the drum, 'charpoy,' a little frayed from over use, fan etc. were in a corner under the tattered jute awning by the side of the outer courtyard. During summers every member of the family laid out mats and slept in the courtyard in front of the 'cooler.'

This household, as the others, in the locality were perpetually busy!

Not only did Shanta manage the endless chores a home required from dawn to dusk, Bindiya was expected to do her share of work too. When their father was at the fields with her brothers, Bindiya helped her mother collect dung/wood, cook, wash clothes, bring utensils, bring water, help clean wheat/ other harvested crops and tend to the cattle too. As children Bindiya or her brothers never thought of going to school! Their responsibilities were totally concentrated on doing backbreaking household tasks and nothing else! Her brothers from early in life were taken to the field to manage odd jobs there, "Learn the ropes my sons! One day 'Maalik,' the land lord, will want to employ you too!" Their father always explained when taking his sons to the farm lands.

The kitchen was an open 'chula' in the inner courtyard. The chula was also hand made. Every six months Shanta, filled a pail with black mud from the fields. She mixed straw into this mud and then slapped it into a rectangular block some inches above the ground. She then bent it on the sides and shaped it so it had a hollow in its centre. Joining the two front ends with a thin foot ruler shaped piece. She made three little mounds to balance cooking pots. Once her handicraft dried, her stove was ready! Inside the hollow dung cakes, wood or even sometimes coal was burnt and cooking pots were placed on top of the mounds. Since it was on the ground, Shanta would sit on her haunches to prepare meals. It was not uncommon to see Shanta desperately blowing, "wohshhhhhhhwohssssss!" Through a cylindrical iron pipe into the lit stove to get a fire going! Stacks of wood and dung cakes were piled near the stove. A few utensils were scattered there; as well as an iron girdle, rolling pin, and a small round wooden 'chakla,' board. Right next to the stove on the weak mud wall, Shanta with the help of a pick, had scratched out a square cavity. Two wooden shelves had been jammed into this cavity. A dirty plastic bottle cut off from the top held salt; opened packets of daily spices lay about in a heap in those shelves. A large plastic bottle of cooking oil, thoroughly coated by grime was near the chula too. Also besides the 'chula' was a pit filled with live coals. Over it sat the milk cauldron. Milk simmered over these coals forever so it seemed to Bindiya. By the end of the day a thick layer of cream would firm over the milk surface. Shanta or Bindiya would skim the cream and collect it in a clay pot; once the cream fermented fresh butter would be churned. Sometimes Shanta heated the cream to make pure 'ghee,' (clarified butter).

Two huge glass urns were used to store the 'ghee.' Butter was stored in a stone pot that had a tight lid. The butter was kept cool by immersing the stone pot in a tub of water.

The children loved to raid the butter pot; especially the boys!

A little away, a tall, black, weather beaten plastic container, with a tap or 'tooti' held water; the container water was used for washing utensils, there was no drain or pipe to conduit off the dirty water used for washing. The water just seeped into the rough floor; letting off a permanent odour that struck the nose every time one passed from there.

Play time over, Bindiya immediately began washing the utensils using water from the plastic container; the water used was raw and bracken; it tasted bad. The source of this water was the village well or the 'talab' or pond; due to the topography of the place this water was bracken. Water, was untreated! 'Sweet' treated water was an indulgence 'Bapu,' father, brought sometimes from the 'Haveli' taps! Drinking slightly salty water that had a dull after taste common for the inhabitants of this village!

A puff of ash powder tickled Bindiya's nose as she mixed mud and ashes from the stove, to use as detergent for the aluminium vessels she was washing. She had filled up an old twisted iron pail with water from the plastic container and she was dipping the utensils in it.

In-spite of pond and the one natural well in the village, water was considered precious and needed to be saved; water irrigating the fields was in an unsaid pact by the villagers not theirs to use freely! Also hygiene played no part in this situation at least. The fact that she was dipping the mud/ash scrubbed utensils in grimy water to rinse them went unnoticed.

"Bindiya, leave the utensils and make dung cakes." Shanta instructed. With in seconds Bindiya had taken charge of the dung basket. Lifting off fodder and hay (lying in heaps next to the 'kotari' door), in the correct portions, Bindiya mixed in the dung and then began to make cakes. She sat at the sunniest part of the outer courtyard and began to shape, slap on dung cakes on to the wall.

Suddenly a head popped up from the low wall, where Bindiya was slapping dung cakes. "Oi…..(giggle)….Laxmi cow chased Ramu chacha again!"

It was Jhumri, Sunheri, the neighbour's daughter. She was Bindiya's play mate and best friend. Usually the two engineered many escapades together and had a giggling session every time their pranks or adventures worked.

Bindiya chortled and stood up, "when?"

"In the morning…he was in the fields and she was irritated, boooomp, she tried to hit him with her head!"

Jhumri for the moment turned into Laxmi and pretended to hit her head just like a cow. Bindiya squealed with laugh.

"*Bindiya!*"

"Oi your Mother…..sheeesh!" Jhumri made a clownish face and wrung her hands dramatically.

Bindiya burst out laughing, but abruptly stopped when Shanta called sternly, "BINDIYA!"

Jhumri ducked and ran off. Her mother would scold her if she knew she was here with Bindiya instead of finishing her chores. Bindiya quickly ran to her mother, she also was scared of annoying her mother.

Shanta sat in the middle of the inner courtyard, where the small round, stone 'atta' (wheat) 'chaki' (grinder) was. This 'chaki' was found in every house hold in the village. Wheat was cleaned then ground in this very ancient motor less 'machine'. Shanta squatted by the 'chaki,' her hands swiftly turning the rotation stick as ground wheat spilled from a snout into the base plate. Taking handfuls of wheat kernels she poured into the hole in the centre of the 'chaki.' The wheat was technically ground between two round stone slabs, rotated by a stout stick (on one side). This looked like an easy task but it was not. It took a lot of energy to rotate the upper heavy stone with the stick.

Shanta would grind just enough wheat to feed her household. A flour mill was present too near the grain sheds, but most villagers preferred their household mill.

"Grrrrd, grrrd ,grrrd" the noise joined the sounds of the day. When Bindiya entered Shanta , legs outstretched and body bend forward, without stopping, complained, "Where were you? Anyhow after the…."

Shanta's voice faded and she covered her head better with the end of her sari (thus making a veil) and stopped grinding, when she saw her husband, (who everyone knew as Deven), enter. Deven's presence was unexpected since he was supposed to be at the fields ploughing. Their two sons, Montu and Bontu, ten and eight were supposed to be with him.

A niggling strain of panic moved within Shanta's heart but was soon put to rest when Deven announced, "I have to escort the tempo carrying sacks of wheat to Shri Girdhari's 'haveli,' (mansion). The tempo is coming and we shall load. I left Montu and Bontu to take care of the fields; Jharna, (farm help), is with them."

Deven, even though was a tiller, felt very honoured that Shri Girdhari, 'Saab,' (boss), used him for odd jobs too. That gave him access to the 'Saab' also. Not that Deven ever used this opportunity to discuss anything with the 'Saab!' He stood struck by muteness around the Shri Girdhari, only answering when spoken too!

Shanta looked visibly relieved at his explanation. An idea came to her and she softly ventured, "Since you are going there… C-can you get water from the tap too?…er sweet water….…..seek permission from er 'Maalik's,' Shri Girdhari, guard and get water….the well water is not so sweet….." Shanta's voice trailed to a hesitant stop. She knew her husband was hard pressed for time so she hesitantly suggested her idea.

Deven thought for a while then slowly worded, "yes…I will ask permission from the guards."

Even as he said the words his heart quivered at the thought of if he would have had to openly ask the landlord for something as menial as drinking water! Luckily the guards were his friend and would allow him to take water from the 'Haveli' tap.

"As a matter of fact why don't you send Bindiya with me.... After delivering the wheat I was walking back anyways since the tempo will not drop me back; Between Bindiya and me we can carry at least four pots of water?" Deven looked quizzically at Shanta, adding "I would have taken Montu or Bontu but today they will have to be at the fields since I have to go to the Mansion...."

Shanta nodded, "Take Bindiya...at least we will get more pots filled this way".

Bindiya, standing nearby, felt she could not breathe. A situation where she *accompanied her father anywhere had never arisen!* Now to go to the 'haveli' which she had not even seen from a distance, then to walk all the way with father who she never really directly interacted with was something of a revolution in her young life. Bindiya looked at her mother to see her reaction to this suggestion.

But Shanta was nonchalant and thought nothing of it. "Bindiya drink milk and go with 'Bapu,' (father). Carry the water pots too." Was all that was commanded! Her first thought was to run and inform Jhumri. But that was not happening. Bapu was waiting right outside the hut.

Gulping her milk down, Bindiya just nodded dumbly when Bapu gruffly asked from the doorway, "Can we leave now?"

Two

Dust swirled up and added to the minor chaos loading wheat sacks into the Tempo. The tempo actually was a mini truck, with no overhead cover at the back. Everyone seemed to be speaking all at once. Bindiya stood a little away with four water clay pots resting near her feet. With so many grown up around she tried to look invisible! Finally the tempo was loaded and Deven beckoned to his daughter to climb in. Squeezing in and somehow managing to place the pots next to herself, Bindiya, too sat on the floor of the truck. Her left side of head and arms pressed against the sacks; her feet bunched up so the pots could fit in. Her father too somehow managed to squeeze in opposite her! A loud shout to the driver had them bumping forward and on their way. Bindiya felt as if every bone in her body was rattling. Thick rivulets of sweat coated her neck and back. Dust, wheat husk tickled her nose. Bindiya pressed her knees nearer to her chin and tried to hold the pots all at the same time! Self consciously she turned her face so not to look directly at her father thus facing the road. Wind carrying outdoor grime smacked her face relentlessly. Bindiya to keep busy began to notice the route to the Havelli. Oh the mango orchards on the side. After sometime she noticed:

Um there comes the cow sheds …ummm now we turn…..tsk tsk—this place is swarming with vehicles! This way Bindiya passed time. After a good one hour of discomfort, the tempo rumbled to a shaky stop.

Deven scrambled off and helped Bindiya dismount. The pots were placed safely in a corner.

Deven then hesitated. He observed the melee of people and shrugged as if realising something. "Bindiya will have to come inside. She cannot be left here." He mentally mused.

"Come with me", Deven said to Bindiya. The tempo with loud rumbles was parked at the entrance of the mansion. From the outside all Bindiya could see was a long unending tall white, solid, cemented wall. A set of metal double doors, painted bright blue broke the surface of the wall. The doors were open and two men instructed Deven to meet 'Maalik,' (big boss), before unloading. Next to the door was a large kiosk. Bindiya curiously stared at the uniformed guards coming in and out of the kiosk. Bindiya did not realise that the kiosk was a guard house that housed four guards for the blue coloured entry doors!

Wiping his face with the end of his shirt, Deven nodded and asked Bindiya to follow him in. "I will not be comfortable leaving you alone here, so come with me. Maintain a respectful silence always and speak only when spoken to." Deven curtly explained to Bindiya. Bindiya gulped and followed her father. No arguments. That is how their relation was. His word was every ones command!

Bindiya gasped, when she entered. Beyond the nothingness that one met outside was a beautiful garden. Central vision imbibed a fountain that splashed water all around. Three manicured lawns bordered the sides and front of where she stood. Flowers ran colour riots in their beds at the brims. Down the middle garden and at the end was a huge swing. A crowd of men stood about the swing. On the swing sat a royal looking man. Shri Girdhari! He was portly and clean shaven; wearing a 'paithani salwar,' loose pyjama's, and a 'kurta,' (shirt). For Bindiya this was a strange dress since population hereabouts dressed either in trousers and shirts or 'dhoti, unstitched cloth worn as a lower and 'kurta.' To Bindiya's mind it was even stranger that Shri Girdhari *was wearing Jewellery*! A thick gold chain encircled his neck and numerous rings adorned his podgy fingers!

Behind him stood a bejewelled head covered lady, his wife presumably. Bindiya blinked when she saw the lady.

In her whole life she had not seen anyone so beautiful! The lady was dressed in a heavily embroidered sari; her neck was garlanded with a bulky gold neckpiece, studded with coloured stones. Thick gold bangles, rings, dangling earrings jingled as she moved.

Two huge electric fans strategically placed, at a distance, on both side of the swing blew fresh air, accompanied by a mild fragrant spray, on the couple! Bindiya to say was spellbound is an understatement! She had never seen something like this! What she did not know that a kit on the fans provided sprinklers thus when the fans were put on, a slight, comfortable, scented, drizzle sprayed from them!

"Look down...touch their feet!" Deven hissed under his breath as they approached the couple. Bindiya forcibly brought her attention back to her father trying not to stare.

"Ahh Deven...come come!" Boomed Shri Girdhari waving a chubby hand at his greetings.

Deven bent his whole body forward in obeisance. Nervously Bindiya tried to also; but was quite clumsy in her efforts. They straightened and stood awkwardly.

"Your daughter?" the lady asked in a patronizing yet cultured voice.

Hearing the grand lady speak, Bindiya got the impression that the lady literally was talking down her snobbish nose yet still giving the sense of being genial, meaning the lady was able to sound disdainful yet not rude all at the same time.

Bindiya receded into a shell of self consciousness at being in the centre of attention; as Deven bashfully nodded. Raising her eyes timorously it was then Bindiya noticed what the lady was doing. From a heavy silver tray held by a servant, she was cracking 'betal nut,' supari, with a silver nutcracker and sprinkling it over tiny 'betal leaves,' (paan), neatly laid out on the tray. Even as she spoke her husband carefully lifted off a leaf and chewed.

"Send her to the kitchen...she has come from far...let her partake a snack. Your 'hisaab,' (accounts), will take sometime." The lady paused, then imperiously commanded, "Billlu take her and ask Ammah-ji to feed her."

Immediately one of the men standing around came forward. Deven smiled ingratiatingly and nodded permission for Bindiya to go with Billu. Swallowing hard trying not to shake, Bindiya followed her escort. Till they were within eye vision Billu remained very polite; his body language denoting total concentration on his instructions. Once they reached the mansion he rudely barked at Bindiya to follow him in. Giving her no time to gape at the huge ornate exterior of the mansion!

Bindiya stepped into the kitchen from the service door and stood transfixed. The flooring was pristine white. Bindiya had never seen anything like this before! The kitchen was swarming with people. When Bindiya could settle her eyes she made out one elderly lady who stood at the helm, two cooks furiously stirring pots and pans and three young maids; scurrying hither thither! The maids wore white 'kameez, salwar,' (pyjamas and long shirt), with aprons. The elderly lady wore a neat, but discoloured nylon sari. Her blouse was faded but very clean. Her hair was completely white. She wore it in a tight bun.

"Ammah-ji (term of respect) here one of the tiller's waif's.. Deven's infact...feed her! 'Madamji' has sent her." Billu indifferently said before ambling off. Bindiya felt her whole body flush with embarrassment. She watched Billu leave her; face melted into a look of panic. "Don't bother about him," the elderly lady said beckoning to Bindiya to come forward. Uncertainly glancing over her shoulders and then back to the elderly lady, Bindiya gingerly complied.

"Call me Ammah-ji...this is my domain!" Ammah-ji chuckled even as she scuffed one of the maids for spilling water from a glass. Bindiya was made to sit on the floor mat thrown in the kitchen corner. Bindiya stared as Ammah-ji opened a humming white cupboard like box, the fridge, and pulled out a bottle. She poured water into a tumbler and handed it to Bindiya. Bindiya almost dropped the tumbler.

She never expected the glass to be so cold! She was in for a bigger shock. When she thirstily drank the water it was chilled! Saucer eyed Bindiya licked her lips and put the glass down. Ammah-ji went to a cupboard pulled out some dry snacks. She arranged them on a plate and placed the plate in front of Bindiya.

Bindiya was overcome with reticence and involuntarily her face began to redden. But Ammah-ji did not seem to notice.

"But before you eat you need to......!" Ammah-ji was about to say something when someone entered the kitchen.

"Ammah-ji I want a coke and some wafers...." boomed a haughty voice.

Bindiya stared at the girl who spoke these words. Most probably her own age, but dressed in expensive clothes. In fact the girl was dressed like a boy....blue jeans, and shirt. Her hair was open. Bindiya was fascinated by her silky stresses. Bindiya just could not believe that anyone could have such soft hair and skin. Wafts of perfume filled the air. This girl was so...so...*clean! Smelt divine!*

The girl carried a stately air of authority in her walk and even how she spoke.

When the girl crossed Bindiya to reach the kitchen counter,

she turned up her nose, skirting around her as you would garbage and spat, "oooey look what the cat brought in.....Ammah-ji she smells like a dirty animal—what is she doing in the kitchen.... oooey!"

Bindiya cowered into her corner; the girl's words searing her feelings; Bindiya felt tears rising, but she pushed them back. She could hear Ammah-ji respectfully mumbling an explanation. But what arrested her attention was another voice that sternly admonished, "Chaya that is no way to talk!"

"Oh ok ...sorry." Chaya shrugged indifferently.

Bindiya saw a young lady very neatly dressed in a sari, square spectacles on her face, enter.

She smiled in apology to Bindiya, however she addressed Chaya, "Chaya no eating without washing your hands." "But ...I washed....!" Chaya protested.

"Chaya it is for your own good, maximum diseases are spread through unwashed hands...so go on, go to the sink and wash up." The lady interrupted her in a firm voice.

Frowning yet knowing she had to obey Chaya went to the single sink. The sink was right next to where Bindiya sat. Bindiya kind of froze....crouching and staring at her plate, trying to be as invisible as ever.

Swinging her head, so her hair bloomed out, Chaya strode past her. With a sulky look at having to do something she thought unnecessary, Chaya turned on the taps of the sink, specifically kept for washing hands. From the corner of her eyes, Bindiya gauged what she was doing. Chaya poured a liquid soap in her palms. Lathering up she rinsed thoroughly. Bindiya's nose was treated to a refreshing fragrance. Hmmmm it smelled so nice. It would smell nice it was hand wash soap but Bindiya did not know that.

Even before Bindiya could assemble their presence in her mind, they left. Ammah-ji had fulfilled Chaya's demands with in seconds. In fact Bindiya noticed how everyone had stiffened to attention.

As soon as Chaya left they all relaxed.

Ammah-ji ignored Bindiya, rummaging through one of the shelves or the other busily. Suddenly she looked at Bindiya,

"Eat what is in front of you now! But before that you need to wash your hands...that's what I was saying before they came.... ugh your hands are filthy."

She signalled to Bindiya to come to the sink, where Chaya had just visited. "Put out your hand Ammah-ji with a wrinkled nose said.

Bindiya stretched her palm. From a distance, so not to contaminate the bottle, so it seemed Ammah-ji squeezed out some soap on to her hand. Asking Bindiya to put water, lather and rinse Ammah-ji then opened the tap. Cold water swished on to Bindiya's hands. What a lovely feeling. Bindiya took a deep breath- her hands smelt divine!

"(Sniff)...*Don't use the towel!*" Ammah-ji with her chin indicated to the white fluffy hand towel hanging on the handrail.

Bindiya wiped her hands on the sides of her dress; even as Ammah-ji observed her!

"Now sit and eat."

Bindiya promptly followed the direction and began to eat. The plate contained 'matri' and 'shaker para,' (Indian savoury and sweetmeats). Ammah-ji turned and began supervising meals, leaving Bindiya alone.

Slowly, Bindiya began to relax. She chewed thoughtfully still sitting cross legged on the floor. She noticed the maids wore something over their regular clothes. Actually they were wearing, as said before, same coloured aprons!

One maid was washing utensils. Bindiya rubbed her eyes and still sitting stretched to see better; the maid was washing in a white bowl like contraption, sink. From two silver faucets water gushed; Bindiya could not believe her eyes. Water effortlessly flowed. Bindiya noticed the maid pour liquid out of a bottle and create soapy foam in a red plastic bowl.

She scrubbed the utensils with this foam. Intermingling with the kitchen smells rose a strong lemony fragrance. After rinsing the maid was stacking the shiny steel dinner plates on to a rack. Ammah-ji, sweeping down to the washing bay, suddenly whacked the maid and held up a plate.

"This one still has not been cleaned properly. It is soapy! How many times do I tell you to leave it under running water so it is thoroughly cleansed...humph...re-wash all of them!"

The maid swiftly took the plate and obeyed.

Bindiya watched, a little amazed how as she, the maid, re-washed all the plates under the gushing tap! Her eyes wandering, Bindiya espied highly polished glass cupboards full of stuff she did not recognise, opposite from where she sat on the floor.

The two cooks were cooking on a table. Bindiya wondered how they were standing, bend over the table, cooking. She had never heard of Gas fuel or four burner gas stoves you see!

"Sigh...Ammah-ji- tea....."

Bindiya whipped her head around; the kind lady who had been with Chaya, re-entered, but this time alone.

"Oh so you are still here little girl!" The lady smiled at Bindiya.

Bindiya responded with a shy smile, bending into her plate furthermore. Her soul however at that moment filled with love for this kind bespectacled lady, who spoke so nicely to her.

"AAh ,"Teacher-ji,"...come, come....make tea for "Teacher-ji", Ammah-ji called to the cook. The cooks were at one end of the kitchen. Where Bindiya was there was a counter and a few chairs too. "Girl move aside and let ""Teacher-ji"" get to the chair...she is Chaya baby's guru...she teaches baby everything... she is a fountain of knowledge!" Now why Ammah-ji said all this was not clear, but it got Bindiya moving; still sitting on the floor Bindiya, by the force of Ammah-ji's words shifted hurriedly, so the teacher could go towards a chair.

"Oh "Ammah-ji stop it…" "Teacher-ji" blushed and settled down in the chair.

Ammah-ji glared at one of the helps and he ran to arrange a tray for tea and help the cook.

Bindiya was consumed by nervousness. But Ammah-ji and the 'teacherji' seemed to have forgotten her in those moments as they talked.

"Ammah-ji please make sure the help, all of them, wash their hands before doing anything in the kitchen. These people don't wash their hands, they don't bathe… they eat with the same filthy hands!" Ammah-ji scurried around listening, but it was Bindiya who turned the battery of full attention to what was being said. Drawing traces on the counter with her fingers the lady continued, "*the result?*…vomiting, upset tummies, and very badly sick or gastro enteritis! OOf it makes me so angry….no education… *they are uneducated yokels*…….can you believe it no one comes to report the case at the hospital… hospitals are places to cure but these people have other ideas!"

Bindiya simply wanted to go up to the teacher and say, "I believe you…..tell me about hospitals.. *If I am ill I will go there because you say so*…." Bindiya wanted to assure this good lady that she Bindiya would emerge as the hope she was looking for! But of course she could not muster courage to interrupt the teacher. Instead she listened intently.

"………they can die" the teacher was speedily saying, at the same time sipping her tea, "yet they have more faith in their quack local medicine men who have no knowledge…." the teacher paused and seemed to withdraw into her own thoughts. Ammah-ji too was silent.

Two threads of emotions intertwined into Bindiya's heart; one of total fascination for this soft spoken 'guru' who seemed so dignified and knowledgeable. The other emotion was that of guilt.

She and her people were a part of the problem the 'Teacherji' was talking about. She or her family had no idea that disease was spread through unwashed hands!

Then like a blanket of unnerving truth, Bindiya remembered most people were afflicted by the sickness the 'Teacherji' spoke of and usually died. Oh no ….*this disease could be prevented just by washing hands?* Bindiya wanted to ask questions but she was so intimidated that she cringed down further.

The teacher began to talk again, "flies…are the worst carriers of disease. But these people never cover their food….God knows where the flies have sat then they sit on the food that is how disease spreads. These people live in such pitiable conditions… open drains. No check on the mosquitoes too, *mosquitoes cause fever*….their awareness is zilch!" She quietly thumbed a balled fist on the counter and continued, "they should come forward and report this…..even if Shri Girdhari knew…he could help. But no…all are so scared! Sigh!" Sipping her tea she added, "I tell him but it never has an impact!"

Bindiya's heart sank. Her village was full of flies…her mind carefully absorbed the teacher's words.

"I, however, long to tour these villages around here and help carry awareness…maybe I will." "Teacherji" voiced her thoughts aloud.

Ammah-ji was nodding and saying,

"Teacherji" this girl is from the slums….far from here…..though I made her wash up she is so dirty she needs a bath badly…..!" Ammah-ji jokingly chuckled.

Suddenly finding attention on herself, Bindiya curled up self consciously.

"Ammah-ji…at least you should not talk like that!" "Teacherji" almost in a scandalized voice hushed the old lady. Ammah-ji shrugged and stood where tea was being prepared her mind furiously thinking: OOf "Teacherji" is so sensitive; I was just joking!

"Child what is your name?" "Teacherji" asked maybe to defuse the unkind situation Bindiya was forced into.

Croaking Bindiya managed to say, "Bindiya"

"Ahhh lovely name…..do you go to school?"

Bindiya stared at the teacher, confused by the question. But she did not have time to answer as her father walked in. He bowed in greetings to the teacher and Ammah-ji, then said, "Bindiya time to leave."

"Deven…..have tea." Ammah-ji offered.

Deven shook his head respectfully, explaining he needed to get back to the fields.

Three

The drinking water tap was on the outside wall of the Mansion's kitchen. Deven had asked permission before leaving and was confidently taking water now.

Deven nudged the pots under the gushing tap and fill all the pots. Meanwhile Bindiya gazed around her. She noticed that at least four young boys were sweeping the garden paths. The fountain was bubbling with water and huge sprinkles swung water into the green lawns. She felt cool and nice. "Pick up the pots." held her father and Bindiya was jolted out of her reverie. She quickly helped her father. Though the water pots were heavy, Deven effortlessly heaved both pots on his head. So did Bindiya; one atop the other. Then in a very rhythmic walk, as marathon walkers do, they made their way back. No words were exchanged.

"Deven…. Deven…stop…listen….going home?" A 'Jugaar,' assembled by what is available, noisily stopped besides them. A 'Jugaar' was an explicit example of invention at its best. The rural populace ingeniously placed a diesel engine on a truck axle and gave it proper truck tires; a body made with wooden planks! The hammered wooden floor at the back assured seating places.

A steering wheel was attached and voila a motorised driving

machine that could withstand all bumpy journeys was created! Dust was whirling up and Bindiya wrinkled her nose and squinted against the afternoon sun to see. The driver, Satish, was grinning; leaning out of the elevated seat, hands still on the protruding steering wheel, speaking to Deven.. "Hop in I am going to the grain sheds... I will drop you off there...come, come.... it will save you some walking at least!"

"Thank you Satish! Bindiya climb in. I will hand you the pots." Deven in a voice tinged with relief said.

Bindiya nodded, and followed her father to the back of the vehicle.

"Ughnm!" Bindiya hastily held the side rails and heaved on to the machine. Her clumsy efforts causing the wooden planks to graze her knees uncomfortably. She noticed the diesel drum squashed against the driver's seat back. A pipe fitted into the engine ensured the flow of fuel! Deven quickly loaded the pots. "Hold them", saying that, he climbed up in the small space next to Satish. The driver's seat was a small wooden board with hardly any space. But that did not prevent Deven from squeezing in! Deven actually had to sit facing the left, legs dangling out, to sit!

"Dug----grdu dugggggggggg!" the machine rumbled, bumped and swayed on its way.

Bindiya, teeth involuntarily chattering by the vibrations of the 'Jugaar,' used her hands and legs to hold the pots steady. Her relief knew no bounds when she reached! Satish dropped them by the grain sheds and from there they resumed walking. Bindiya's legs felt wobbly and she thought, "I prefer walking than that "jugaar"!

In sometime they reached home. Bindiya hesitated by the lane entry. She stared at her lane. What was different?

"Girl...why have you stopped? Come. *Deposit the water*..." her father's voice interrupted her as he walked ahead.

Almost visibly shaking herself, Bindiya treaded her way home.

The dogs lazily resting by the drain did not get the usual reaction from her this time. She bleakly absorbed the dirty drain, and scruffy environs, with dismay percolating her emotions for some unexplainable reasons! Her father reached first and allowed his wife to help him unload the pots. Likewise Shanta helped Bindiya. The water pots were placed in a corner of the inner courtyard.

"I was expecting you a little later...you are earlier than I thought?" Shanta smiling said.

"Yes we were fortunate to get a lift...I am glad...I don't know how we would have crossed the road on the busy high way carrying the pots!" Deven chuckled.

It was early evening, the sun still not set. Montu and Bontu were chattering nineteen to a dozen. They lay stretched in the courtyard. Bindiya had no time to play. She had to finish certain chores then help Shanta prepare the evening meal. Deven was chatting to a neighbour right outside the front door. Coming in he shouted, "Cut the water melon I brought in the morning!"

Deven had been given the water melon by a farmer friend.

Obeying, Bindiya extracted a huge water melon left in a pail full of water. The arrival of the water melon earlier in the morning had sent a thrill of anticipation through the children. "Montu fill a pail and dip the fruit!" Bapu had said bringing in the green weighty fruit into the hut! Montu ran off to the well to get a pail of water! The watermelon was put into water to cool it. Now heaving it out of the pail and walking in a bent swagger, Bindiya placed it on the floor next to the stove. Picking up the sharp knife Bindiya hesitated. The knife lying near the stove had a dozen flies buzzing over it. "Flies carry maximum disease" 'Teacherji's' voice rang in Bindiya's head. Bindiya noticed that the knife had not been wiped earlier, after a vegetable had been cut. Bindiya shook the flies off, wiped the knife with the hem of her frock and began to cut the water melon into wedges. Putting all the slices into a steel plate she walked up and placed it on a mat. "Come on eat!" she called her brothers. This was a signal. Shanta, Deven, Montu, Bontu and Bindiya sat cross legged and devoured the fruit. Munching and spitting out the black seeds Montu commented "I love this fruit!" Trickles of juice ran down his chin, inviting a laugh from Bapu. Bontu giggled too making gurgling noises as the juice of the fruit filled his mouth and ran down his chin.

Bindiya giggled extending a bowl so everyone spat the seeds into it. Shanta would dry the seeds and grind them to powder. This powder was eaten through out summers to battle the heat.

Dusk arrived and then finally it was bedtime. They all dutifully rubbed mustard oil mixed with neem leaves all over their body to ward off mosquitoes. Shanta then burnt leaves and some strong herbs to 'smoke' out the vampire mosquitoes swarming the place. Since, the electricity was so fickle they burnt oil lamps. Earlier Bindiya had carefully filled oil in two lamps. She placed one near the stove. The other was kept outside to go to the fields with.

The lamp's flickering light only added to the dark gloom of the night. Bindiya for the first time in her young life felt some difficulty in getting sleep.

Bindiya felt a rising frustration in her heart. She felt it all evening. Why was she suddenly noticing how dirty everything around her was? She could not explain it; but suddenly the room she slept in smelt. Her mother turned and the puff of body odour made Bindiya wrinkle her nose.

Bindiya placed her hands over her nostrils trying to bring back the scent of the soap she had used there. Even as she did that, the heady scents of Shri Girdhari's mansion filled her memory..involuntarily she smiled…drowsiness overcoming her abruptly……they are so…um….clean…were the last thoughts as sleep claimed her senses.

"*Bindiya* go help Jhumri to clean the drain, it has choked again!" Shanta flipped a thick 'roti' on the hot gridle as she shouted to her daughter next morning. Bontu and Montu giggled loudly seeing Bindiya face fall at this order.

"What are you laughing at huh?" Bindiya snapped at the two.

"Giggle...ha ha ha ...smmmmmmmerrf" The boys sitting cross legged in front of their breakfast plates sniggered, their mouths full of food! However, Shanta mildly admonished them,

"Hush....go do as you are told...boys no teasing!"

Frowning at her brothers teasing her, Bindiya stepped out of the hut.

Bindiya had been dying to tell Jhumri about her jaunt to the haveli and about Chaya's hoity-toity ways. Yet today Bindiya was just not up to it.

Four

Almost with an expression of disdain and reluctant beating heart, Bindiya grabbed the long stick and went out. At the end of the lane she saw Jhumri bent over the mouth of the drain…plodding and poking too with a stick.

The drain had greyish stagnant water and the stink was unbearable. A swarm of mosquitoes puffed up as they opened the choke. The mosquitoes had company, flies. This was not uncommon.

"Bad na?" Bindiya muttered to Jhumri.

"Oh yes yuck waste, husk, leaves and cannot imagine what has choked it. Aaaargh these stupid mosquitoes!"

"Here let me." Bindiya used her stick to prod the choked outlet; Jhumri stood aside. Jhumri helpfully brushed aside the mosquitoes and flies. This was a common problem and the children of the lane were usually deputed to clear it!

Bindiya knew that this drain was also used as a toilet by the younger kids. The very thought made her dizzy! What was wrong with her? Before this she never had a problem cleaning the drain but today it seemed her nostrils would burst with the stink. "Oh ..this is terrible…I hate it…why do we have to do this…yuck. I don't want to do this!""

Jhumri giggled and teased, "really?.. you don't want to do this?…Bindiya…are you a queen? This is our chore…what's your problem…ha ha ha!"

Bindiya wanted to share her experience at the mansion, but seeing Jhumri's amused face she shrugged and continued to clean the drain.

Lifting off unrecognisable filth Bindiya again felt her frustration rise. But somehow she could not put words to it.

"There…pull that plastic bag…..yech…what is that?" Jhumri mumbled as Bindiya pronged something and pulled it out and deposited on the outer side of the drain.

It never occurred to either of them to pick up the filth from where they were depositing. The heap of garbage collected from the drain would rot besides it for days!

"AHHH…you did it …it has opened… water is flowing in the drain." Jhumri chortled in a relieved tone.

Bindiya did not answer; a giddy spell attacked her again. Slowly she made her way back to the house.

Jhumri called after her, "lets play hide and seek in the evening… with Montu, Bontu and my sisters and brothers." Jhumri's face crumpled slightly, "Oh no Chotu, her younger brother, has fever and he is vomiting" Jhumri's expression changed as she said, "But never mind we still can play…Bindiya…Bindiya."

Jhumri called since Bindiya seemed to be preoccupied and had not really heard the conversation properly! With some difficulty Bindiya turned her attention back to her friend, muttering,

"What?"

"Let us all play hide and seek this evening?" Jhumri hopefully repeated.

Oh alright…I will..let me go home now!" Bindiya snapped. "Promise?"

"Ok ok.. promise." Bindiya's irritated tone was obvious, but

Jhumri was an easy, happy go lucky person and she did not pick up the negative vibes; brightly scuttling back to her own home without a care in the world!

When Bindiya returned home, Shanta was standing by the door, in her hands was a basket of full of semi-dried dung cakes, "Bindiya go dry these with the others. Sheila bhabhi is down with high fever she cannot go with you so take her basket too."

"Mosquitoes cause fever…." danced in Bindiya's mind. Her insides churned and she wanted to refuse her mother the task; instead talk about what she had overheard the 'Teacherji' say at the Haveli. She could not.

Hiding her expression, Bindiya took the basket from her mother.

"Ufff-I hate this" Bindiya grumbled dropping the basket as she stopped at a field. A square tract of land was neatly, albeit, completely covered with dung cakes, stationed in neat rows. With a sigh Bindiya added her fresh load to the rows as well. Once done she walked back home.

When Bindiya entered her house, she stopped in front of her mother,

"Mother I am going to the well …I want to bathe."

"Bathe? Are you mad…you bathed day before…water is precious…bathe..humph! Help me here to cook." Her Mother without turning around, still sitting on her haunches said.

Bindiya never contradicted her mother but today something within her moved to do so, "Mother I feel dirty…I am going to bathe." She said the last words firmly.

Shanta's jaw dropped and she fully turned to stare at Bindiya. Bindiya 's attention was reverted to the flies buzzing over the dough her mother had just kneaded.

Even as her mother was speaking, Bindiya picked up an aluminum plate to cover the dough.

Shanta paused, then, looked at the covered dough, then, at

Bindiya, up and down. She took a sharp in take when Bindiya turned and walked away; with a rapidly beating heart gathering courage, to mutter, "Flies carry disease."

"Ack?" Her Mother stared after her wondering why her daughter was grumbling and what was she saying?

Bindiya did not wait, she went into the room and pulled out a frayed towel. She owned only two frocks. She knew she was too old to be in frocks but her slight built did not make it look odd. Mother had begun mentioning that Bindiya needed to wear 'Salwar' and 'Kameezes,' pyjamas and long shirt. Every now and then Shanta reminded everyone in general that next shopping trip Bindiya's wardrobe needed a drastic change! Bindiya did not mind wearing frocks. Even Jhumri still wore them, for them there was no vanity involved in their choice of clothes.

Presently Bindiya pulled out her other frock. Both the frocks were quite tattered and sewed over and over again. However next month her father and mother would be visiting the 'haat,' (bazaar), in the city and dutifully clothes would be purchased for the children. Bindiya found a tiny piece of soap, her comb and a hand mirror. Deven used this mirror when he shaved. Bindiya bundled everything into the towel.

Without looking towards her mother, she stepped out and made her way to the well. She could feel her mother's eyes boring into her back.

The well was isolated. With expertise of long practise, Bindiya threw the pail in and pulled out water. There were two empty pails lying there already, Bindiya filled them to the brim, including the third pail she was using.

Behind a thick hedge that acted like a screen Bindiya carried the pails. She took a bath; the silver of soap hardly a good cleanser. When Bindiya finished bathing and was dressed she washed her frock as best she could. Spreading it over the side of the well she then propped the mirror and began to comb her hair. "O wow eeesssh yeow!" Bindiya yelped at the pain the comb caused her! The comb was useless on her knotty rough hair. Sometimes Shanta sat, behaving as if she had to resign to a very big task of unknotting Bindiya's hair. Today Bindiya did not feel like taking any help. Bindiya really never had time for hair treatment.

In frustration Bindiya threw the comb away. Her eyes rested on her feet. Bindiya felt tears brimming. Her feet were still black with the muck she collected whilst walking; the rough plastic slippers she wore gave hardly any protection. Bindiya stared at her hands and dirty under nails. Picking up the mirror she gazed at her face. The bracken water of the well had not really freshened her. Her torn dress and grimy towel saddened her.

She closed her eyes and the vision of her mind. Chaya's soft hair, fragrance, clean home, mapped an insistent teasing reminder again and again.

She even remembered the fragrant soap and white fluffy towel kept on the side of the sink. A bubble of frustration cried…"I want to be like her!"

"What is the matter with you Bindiya?" Shanta almost spat. "Why are you running the utensils under the 'tooty,' (tap)… wasting precious water…fill that bucket and rinse….!"

Bindiya had returned home and had immediately been sucked into the daily industry of housework!

"Ma….the bucket water turned grey…we cannot keep washing with the same water again and again…" Bindiya said, still holding a plate under the trickling water from the black plastic container. "Stop that…..who will fill water…..!" Shanta almost hysterically shrieked.

Sullenly Bindiya stopped and sat a little away from the utensils. Her eyes travelled to Shanta's exposed ankle since Shanta sat on her haunches and swept the courtyard. An ugly weal travelled from Shanta's heel to her ankle bone. This was the result of an accident where Shanta had fallen off the bullock cart and hurt her ankle. Dayaji had been consulted.

The cut was so deep that it needed stitches. Dayaji had taken an ordinary needle, burnt its tip on fire to sterilize it and used some thread to stitch the cut.

Shanta had developed fever and was in a bad way. Shanta's own strong will pulled her through. It was quite a crisis and Bindiya who was just seven-years-old thought her mother was going to die! Our body heals naturally too and maybe that is what Shanta's body did. She was very, very lucky. The wound slowly healed but the welt was still there. It wound tight around the heel and ankle and gave Shanta a permanent pain. Even now Shanta bit her lips as she squatted and swept.

Dayaji. At this point it would be prudent to give a brief character sketch of the man who seemed to be controlling the health department of the village! Dayaji was not an evil witch doctor as one would like to believe. He was a meek man who found his power over people in dispensing natural medicines. He ventured into this practise years ago, had a few successes that gave him the 'good healer' tag of the medicine man!

He *did* know his job of ancient medicine from herbs and roots however over the years his methods contrasted sharply with the needs of the changing times. Somewhere down the line Dayaji began to develop a rigid and obdurate attitude towards any other medication but his own.

His offhand disparaging remarks about regular doctors and hospitals made a big impact on the simple villagers. They did not want to have anything to do with those faceless doctors at big hospitals so far off! Yes.

They agreed with Dayaji who always cautioned to "trust the one you know!" For them he seemed the only solution to their ills! Dayaji did not mind this at all. His patronising, 'I know everything' demeanour acted like a comfort potion for the dwellers of hereabout and gave him a superior air!

"What has happened to you....are you sick?" Shanta, broke into her thoughts and frustrated, cried; as she became aware that her daughter was staring at her.

Bindiya felt anger rise within her; unable to stop herself, she stormed out of the house. Once out she began to run. She ran towards the tree in the clearing. Without stopping her pace she sprung forward and grabbed the tire 'swing' tied high up to the tree. This swing was made with two thin cycle tires tied together. It had been put up for the children. Grabbing the tires tight Bindiya curled up her legs and like a pendulum swung for a while. She did a half roll, a spin and then with vengeance back and forth sway. The whole exercise calming her somehow! With the click of her tongue Bindiya jumped off and flopped to the ground.

Why was she feeling so angry? A million thoughts related to the 'Haveli' visit replayed in her mind. She rose and began to walk.

She was deep in thoughts; little realising she was walking towards the fields. It took sometime but Bindiya hardly noticed. The "chuk chuk" of the tube wells welcomed her. Tillers were busily ploughing the fields. Four buffaloes were rotating a wheel constructed over a well and generating water from a tank to irrigate the fields. There was a tube well there also. Water was being siphoned out of the tube well by noisy diesel generated pumps. She noticed her father at a distance too. Ignoring all she climbed the platform around the tank. Hidden by the axle wheel and to some extent the grunting buffaloes, Bindiya sat there for a long time. It was shady so the sun did not bother her. Usually Jhumri accompanied her; today Bindiya just did not feel like meeting anybody.

She stared at the buffaloes, heavily yoke led turning around and around. That is us.....dirty.....bonded buffaloes! Bindiya abruptly thought. This thought shook her and she bit her lip. In an involuntary moment she cupped her hand and drank water from the tube well tank. She left the fields and walked to the 'talab' or water pond. Flopping down on the cool grassy bank, Bindiya saw a few village women washing their clothes. Two boys were swimming and six buffaloes were bathing too. For the cows, buffaloes and humans to use the same water tank did not seem strange in rural areas. Bindiya did not think much of it. She sat and just whiled her time. "Dhook, dhook, dhook!" the tractor maneuvered on to the path from the field. It was the end of the growing season for wheat and the crop had been cut.

Of late Shri Girdhari had got the machine called thresher; The thresher was a farm machine for separating seeds or grain from the husks and straw. The dry straw taken away as bedding etc. for the animal sheds and the seeds or kernel was collected.

Lazily Bindiya marveled at the thought that wheat grew to such abundance from a seed. First a green sprout that developed a head which was full of seeds, in to golden plant to light brown in colour! It would harden and dry. That was when it was harvested. Wheat had been sowed in spring and harvested now in summer. Now after the harvest, the fields were being prepared for other crops! The same field in rotation sowed different principal crops. The tractor would be attached with a 'drill' that would plant the seeds and dig long rows for it! The farm lands never rested. They were forever being prepared for a crop. "What a busy life this land has!" Bindiya chuckled to herself. Her mind wandered and she thought about what the teacher at the Haveli had said. Unease filled her heart. Bindiya thought, "Suddenly I am noticing things…I don't want to hurt Ma, or sound like a snob! But we really need to become clean. The Haveli was spic and span…no wonder Chaya thought I was dirty and stank like an animal! No one ever rejected me like that. Sigh! I learnt that to be clean one has to make efforts. We can do it here too…*why doesn't anyone understand that it is important to be clean.* No one is going to listen to me; helplessness infused her being.

Her thoughts propelled her feet to towards a large tract of land circled by a tree line Bindiya stopped as she spotted her brothers scampering on the trees with two other boys. They were having an 'ulat' competition!

This was a trick the children had mastered was a backward flip to climb trees. They even invented a name and called it the 'ulat,' (backward flip). 'Ulat,' actually was specific to the children of this village only! All trees got an 'ulat' from one child or the other!

"Press your back tight against the trunk of the tree; stretch your hands up, grasp a low branch and effect a neat summersault and land on a higher branch." Was the training giving to a curious novice anytime he or she wanted to effect an 'ulat!'

After many grazed, bruised elbows, knees and foreheads, the trick was perfected! Bindiya of course had not done an 'ulat' for a long time. When she was younger it was her favourite method of plucking fruit! For awhile Bindiya enjoyed watching the boys. Then, she sighed and abruptly turned homewards.

Shanta, did not say anything when Bindiya re-entered the hut. But Bindiya arrested her own stride and surveyed her surroundings. Where would she start in order to begin the clean up drive? Was the only deliberation bustling in her psyche!

"Ma….let us clean this   'Kotari,'   (store)…look   at the cob webs…can I go borrow the big, tall broom from Sunheri chachi's house?" Bindiya hopefully asked the next morning.

"Clean the store? Why? No, no….you go and make stacks of the twigs and wood I have got for the stove."

"B-ut Ma…"

Shanta gave Bindiya a strange look but said nothing. She picked her bundle of clothes to wash and left for the 'talab,' (pond).

What has got into the girl? Shanta's mind buzzed as she sauntered on. Bindiya was so quiet in the morning too…hmm this girl! I don't know what her problem is! Soon Shanta joined the group of other ladies going to the water pond and her mind wandered away from Bindiya and her rebellious attitude!

"Bindiya!" Jhumri, in a woebegone voice called her.

"Jhumri..." Bindiya nodded and ran to talk over the low wall where she could see Jhumri's head popping up.

"Jhumri you are looking so white...no rather green.. like you are sick or something....what is it? What happened?"

"Nothing...Ma says touch of sun....she says no to time off from the household work...sigh I feel pretty ill though!! Chotu is unwell too...." There was a tired, brusque tinge to her tone too.

Bindiya glanced up at her startled and was about to ask what was wrong with Chotu when,

"Jhumri!"

Sunheri's voice hollered from somewhere at the back.

"Bindiya I have to go....see you later..!" Jhumri's head disappeared.

Bindiya shrugged and flopped right there at the low wall. She did not feel like doing anything. The teacher's and Chaya's words revolved round and round in her head. She lost herself in an imaginary world where she was clean and smelling good... everyone was treating her with dignity!

When Shanta returned Bindiya was still sitting. Shanta scowled at her and in an angry voice demanded her to get up and finish her jobs, "the twigs/wood is lying scattered....you have not stirred the milk cauldron......." Bindiya stared wide eyed at her mother. Angry words spewed uncontrollably from Shanta's mouth. To Bindiya mind all words merged into one, to sound like a hollow groan from a trumpet, "gnawwwwwwww!"

She could not make out one word her mother said. Shaking these thoughts off as one would droplets of rain and deeply sighing, she abruptly stood up. Shanta startled by her sudden movement was quiet. Bindiya ignoring these reactions, as if nothing had happened returned to her chores. Licking her lips and somehow feeling deflated, Shanta followed her inside. Refraining from nagging further, Shanta began drying the clothes she had washed at the pond.

As dusk fell, Bindiya reluctantly applied the mosquito oil. "It makes me stink like an animal." Bindiya said in her mind the words of Chaya still ringing in her mind; still feeling smelly Bindiya, after dinner, squatted by the milk cauldron. Milk had thickened and was creamy. And the coals embers were dying. With the ladle she poured milk into four steel glasses. From an opaque plastic bottle, with the help of a spoon, she dropped sugar into the hot milk. Using a flat aluminium plate as a tray she carried the milk to where the family was sitting in the inner courtyard. Taking their milk they all sat restfully sipping with loud slurps. This was their daily routine.

Bindiya too sat with the milk glass cupped in her hands. Sipping slowly, unexpectedly her mind remembered Jhumri. Why was Jhumri looking so-so white? Oh no....was Jhumri really ill or was she angry with me? What was wrong with Chotu?" this idea manifested in her mind making her think hard. "Hmmmmm...*that is why she was looking so ragged and stiff*... I am sure she was angry because I forgot to play..... I have never seen her like that...but I myself have never behaved like this...," This thought tortured Bindiya, even when she went inside to sleep. Chewing her lower lip and staring up at the shadowy outlines of the straw roof beams, Bindiya mused, "Tch tch...I completely forgot, Jhumri had asked me to play hide and seek yesterday? But why did Jhumri not come to remind me? She tried to tell me but her mother called her. Bindiya smiled to herself thinking of how miffed Jhumri looked. No worries, I will make up for it...tomorrow I will tell Jhumri all about my adventure at the Haveli..giggle....so funny how that Chaya talks...Jhumri must have felt bad....I will make her laugh..... Bindiya toyed with these thoughts even as her eyes grew heavy with sleep.

Five

The next morning, Bindiya was woken as usual by her mother at-dawn. "You have to go to the water pond with the ladies, since I have to accompany Bapu to the fields. I cannot wash clothes. Here take these clothes and wash them." She then added, "Pluck 'bhutta's,' (corn on cobs), and bring them back when you return." Shanta's tone was brusque. Knowing she had no choice, even without rinsing her face, Bindiya collected the bundle, washing soap and washing board from its place in a corner and waited at her doorstep. Soon four ladies came out of their huts calling, "Bindiya come!"

Sunheri was present too in the group. Bindiya looked over her shoulders to see if Jhumri was coming.

"Jhumri is not coming. She has to stay home." Sunheri informed Bindiya seeing her searching eyes.

"But why?"

Sunheri did not answer. However, some one had obligingly broken Neem sticks from the tree. She handed them around for them to chew as they walked.

When they reached, they chose their places by the edge of the water pond. Placing a shirt on the board, after soaking it in the pond, Bindiya wet the soap and began to scrub the shirt. The yellow bar of washing soap was cheap, so not much lather built up. When the washing was over they again bundled the wet clothes. Their clothes would be dried at home. Bindiya left her wet bundle and raced to the adjoining maize field. Sprouts of jacketed corn shook their ears merrily as a slight breeze rose. These corn on cobs would be roasted over an open fire, smeared with lemon juice and spices! But Bindiya was preoccupied. She was immune to the weather or the amazing picture of the peeping sun, its rays splintering like a million shards of glass through the floating clouds in the fresh morning sky; and yes in the most friendliest manner throwing dabs of light to where Bindiya stood, surveying which cobs to pluck.

The ladies with her also came to pick some maize. It was then Bindiya overheard Sunheri,

"She has been unwell for the week! I thought it was the sun...... she was fine in the morning though the purging and vomiting continued....now fever....her vomiting has not stopping....she is talking nonsense.....Dayaji, the local medicine man, will make her better! Poor, poor Jhumri!"

Bindiya felt her heart sink. She parted the stalks of corn and reached Sunheri,

"Chachi, (aunt), what is the matter with Jhumri?"

"Nothing. Just a little stomach problem. Dayaji is going to treat her. She will be fine."

"And Chotu?" Bindiya asked hesitantly.

"Chotu he is fine.....Dayaji is taking care," Sunheri nervously answered looking here and there.

"Please....take her...Jhumri...to a hospital...she may n..." Bindiya words were cut off seeing Sunheri's expression.

Sunheri scowled, bunched her three fingers on top of her head; to pull the sari head cover back from her face; and said in disbelief, "what? Bindiya don't speak like a fool...she will be fine...

no hospital!"

Then Sunheri, a little rudely, turned making it clear that she did not want to talk.

Bindiya ran up to her and insisted, " Take her to the hospital... please."

Sunheri by now was very irritated, "Bindiya, what is this stupid behaviour? Hospital? Hospital? A young girl? I, admit to the hospital? To be shown to male doctors? Bah!"

"Chachi believe me they will make her alright please..... listen."

"No. You listen, your mother has been telling me you are behaving strangely and have become rude and overbearing."

Bindiya's eyes amplified with astonishment!

"Yes. Shanta may take your rudeness but not me. So stop arguing do you hear?"

Bindiya blinked then in order to stabilise the conversation; in a somewhat pleading tone asked,

"Forget Ma. You tell me, can I come to your place...meet her...Jhumri that is....is she very sick?"

Now Sunheri turned to stare at Bindiya. In normal circumstances being told off would have meant Bindiya looking chastised and apologetic! But that did not seem to be happening here. Bindiya behaved as if the scolding had no effect on her.

Very angry, Sunheri stormed off, tersely saying,

"No....please *do not* come home....she is er...let her recover...!"

"Why is she behaving so strangely? Is Jhumri sicker than Sunheri Chachi is trying to say?" Bindiya still not catching the: 'I am really angry, signals from Sunheri. Bindiya occupied her own mind with only one worry that is Jhumri's health; all the way back home.

"Did you get the corn?" Shanta asked her as soon as she entered.

Bindiya bit her lip. In the stress of hearing about Jhumri she had forgotten to pluck corn.

Mother….er…Jhumri is very ill….c-can I go see her?"

Shanta glowered at her daughter. Never had she ever forgotten a chore. Shrugging Shanta nodded. Somehow churning butter out of cream seemed a more onerous task then taking her daughter to task at that moment.

Bindiya ran down the road.

"Sunheri chachi…chachi… CHAICHEEEEE!" "Yes?" a head popped from the low wall. It was Jhumri's older brother.

"Can I meet Jhumri?" Bindiya indicated to the latched front door to be opened.

"Er..no….she is not well…come tomorrow." His face looked uncomfortable as he said these words.

Bindiya was shocked. Never had she been denied entry before.

Embarrassedly Jhumri's brother ducked out of sight.

And reluctantly Bindiya returned home. Once again her day unfolded and she lost herself into her world of errands and chores.

"Mangoes. Put them in a pail of water." Deven told Bindiya. Deven emptied the sack of mangoes next to her. "I need the sack." He brusquely explained more to himself than her; thus folding the now empty sack and tucking it under his arm pit.

Bindiya had just returned from the fields. Shanta was blowing at the stove with a 14 inches cylindrical iron pipe. "Cough… cough….ashtooo!" Shanta went.

Deven glanced at his wife but did not offer to help. Bindiya lifted up the hem of her frock and collected the mangoes into the hollow her frock made. Dumping them in the washing area, she filled a pail from the black container and immersed the mangoes. Bindiya usually was so excited when Bapu began bringing mangoes home. The green "langada aam" was an integral part of the mango eating sessions with the family. The season for "langada" had not yet started but he had got "Dusseri" mango. No knives were used. Squeezing from the bottom sharp teeth bit off the top and the pulp sucked out. "trrrrrrrkkkkkkkkkkshrrrrumpop" Bontu would suck. Montu would make a bigger sound…Bindiya would beat him by a louder sound. The entire house would fill with giggles and teasing. So what if pulp messed their faces and dress and hands it was a mango after all! Today Bindiya sulkily washed the mangoes. The fact that they were first of the season did not affect a reaction from her. Finishing she peered up at the sun. Hot days are here…..Bindiya knew the dry dust and hot wind called 'loo' would hit them soon. Walking into the kotari, Bindiya picked up a sickle stuck into a wooden block. "Do I have to cut all the spinach leaves?" Bindiya asked Shanta indicating to the pile of spinach still in the used dung basket. Shanta was still trying to get the stove going, replied between coughs, "cough….I hate this smoke…cough…yes cut all the leaves"

Shanta and Bindiya, at their sojourns at dawn had plucked spinach from a field. Bindiya lifted the entire spinach and kept it besides her mother the she sat down next to her mother and pressed the sickle down with her foot. Collecting the leaves she began to cut the spinach finely.

Bontu and Montu fought. It was all over the last piece of mango. Montu punched Bontu then Montu pushed Bontu. Bindiya tried to extricate on of them from a death lock they had created with their arms and legs. Laughing and shouting Bindiya failed miserably. She did not hear the call at the door that is why. It was only later she saw Deven and Shanta had left the 'fight' in between and had been out in the lane. Just as she managed to tear the boys apart their parents entered. They looked very serious. Shanta not saying anything began to pick up the dirty dishes. She held the corner of her sari veil in her teeth as she worked. Deven lay down on the rope bed and stared at the skies. The boys had sorted out their differences and were sitting in a corner discussing how they would make new kites to play with!

"Ma…what …where were you?" Bindiya asked her mother as they still squatting cleared the lunch dishes. Shanta pressed her ankle to ease pain and answered in a preoccupied way, "nothing.. Sunheri" Shanta thought of something then just dismissed it with a …".nothing."

"Ma what about Sunheri chachi?"

"Jhumri is unwell…"Shanta clicked her tongue and her tone changed to a whine, "I really don't want to talk to you…you were very rude to Sunheri the other day…babbling about hospitals… my own child so rude…"

"Ma let that be…..Is it very serious?"

Shanta was slightly shaken at Bindiya's curt dismissal and maybe a wee bit frightened of the authoritative way she spoke. She found herself answering promptly,

"Nothing just a stomach problem….she wanted me to pluck neem leaves…"

"Neem leaves?"

"Uh uh ….Dayaji is there and she needed to be home….her husband and sons are still at the fields….she will be alright…just an upset stomach."

"Ma….c-cant they take her to a hospital?" Bindiya tentatively inquired.

"Arrrey are you mad? Jhumri will be fine…tell me when did the boys stop fighting?" Shanta abruptly changed the subject wondering why she was having this conversation at all!

Bindiya was about to say something but eventually forgot as she filled her mother with the details of the 'mango fight!'

It was the middle of the night. A loud scream made Bindiya sit up on her mat. What had disturbed her? Where are Ma and Bapu? She stared at their empty mats. Rising Bindiya stumbled over the 'water surai,' urn. She caught it just in time. Adjusting her eyes to the dark, Bindiya left the room and tentatively walked to the front door. She peered down the lane.

"I can hear voices coming from Jhumri's hut. What is the matter? I need to find out. Swiftly Bindiya ran towards the hut. The lane dogs ignored her as did she. Bindiya's heart sank as she neared the hut. She could hear Sunheri wailing and soft murmurs from her mother could be heard too.

Seeing her, Sunheri, cried, "You wanted to know about your friend na? Your friend is sick. She is vomiting and purging. She is so sick. She does not speak…'hai hai,' oh dear- oh dear" She repeated wringing her hands. "Hush!" Shanta consoled her"

Shaken beyond words Bindiya hardly could speak. Her eyes travelled to Jhumri. Jhumri, lay pale and wretched lay in the outer courtyard. Her eyes rolled in some kind of pain. The village medicine man, Dayaji who made his medication from herbs and roots, was burning a few herbs next to her. He was grinding something on the rough floor muttering something all the time.

Deven stood aside with Jhumri's father.

"Why don't you take her to the hospital?"

No one heard her that is Bindiya. Sunheri kept crying. Her husband still stood and stared. Ma and Bapu concentrated fully on Dayaji. Jhumri's siblings, four of them, stood in a terrified huddle. Jhumri appeared not be aware of any one. She moaned in pain.

Bindiya felt anger rising this time she almost shouted, "Take her to the hospital you uneducated yokels! She is going to die otherwise! This man is a fraud….he is not a doctor…….listen to me… take her quickly…."

A shocked silence met her words. Slowly everyone turned to stare at her, including Dayaji who stopped grinding and glared at her. Deven was furious. He purposefully strode up and yanked her by the arm speaking seething, "go home you rude girl…go!" He pushed Bindiya roughly out of the house.

In tears, Bindiya went home. She gritted her teeth in anger.

When she slept she did not know however loud wails woke her up at dawn. Hardly able to breathe Bindiya rushed out.

"Poor thing died," were the first words she overheard a neighbour, part of a huddle standing in the lane, say.

Bindiya felt her throat choke. Pushing through everyone, she skedaddled into the hut.

Her heart sank. Jhumri was dead. Everyone was crying and wailing. Bindiya ran in and stared at Jhumri's lifeless body lying in the centre of the courtyard. Flies buzzed around her face.

Bindiya's face contorted in pain and she shrieked, "you killed her…..you killed her….you killed her."

She was not conscious of the slaps her father Deven rained on her or that her mother helped to drag her away. They threw Bindiya into the store room and pressed the door shutting the entrance. Bindiya slumped on the floor. She felt her heart would break. "Jhumriaaaaa" Bindiya screamed. The dark, filthy room held no comfort. No one came to her.

Six

"It is good Sunheri, will leave with the children for her 'maika,' (parents place), for two days after the funeral...it will take time for them to reconcile the loss of a daughter. Jhumri's last rites...I mean funeral, are to be at their ancestral village right?"

"Yes. That is not far. They have already left." Bindiya heard her father say.

"Sigh! Who can argue with fate?" Shanta's voice came clearly to Bindiya. Bindiya could see them through the chink in the door. It was late evening. Bindiya was still locked up.

"She is behaving so strangely....Bindiya I mean."

Bindiya strained her ears but could not make out anything since her mother had lowered her voice.

Suddenly the door of the 'kotari' was transferred to one side. Deven's silhouette shadowed the entrance.

"Go....eat food...!" He rudely ordered Bindiya.

"I am going to the fields," Deven informed his wife. 'The fields' literally meant going to the fields, to use them as toilets. There were no proper toilet facility systems in these settlements.

Bontu nudged Montu when Bindiya raggedly made her way out.

Shanta coldly slammed her plate down saying "eat".

Bindiya ignored her. She went towards the outer court yard and sat against the wall.

Shanta was amazed at her rudeness. Angrily, she pulled her sari veil tighter over her head and began to shout at Bindiya.

Ugly words poured. Bindiya physically closed her ears to shut the words out.

Suddenly Shanta who had come to the door-less entrance, propelled by her anger, stopped. She could not believe Bindiya had shut her ears. Slumping to the ground Shanta began to wail, *"my daughter had been possessed by a ghost....waaaaahhhhh!"*

Montu and Bontu cried along with her.

Bindiya uncovered her ears and glared at them. Deven rushed in, "Shanta quiet!"

That had an electric effect. Shanta quietened, so did the boys.

Deven turned to Bindiya and looked at her piercingly, "What is the matter with you?"

Bindiya could not believe that she was not scared. Clearing her throat she said,

"We should have taken Jhumri to the hospital."

"Hospitals are all nonsense." Deven dismissed curtly adding."More over we have no way to travel good two hours to the district...then further towards the city....so stop this nonsense. Dayaji is perfectly capable. It is unfortunate Jhumri died but that is the way life is."

"He—he, Dayaji... has killed more then cured." Bindiya blurted.

Deven face went crimson. Shanta and the boys eyes widened and they cringed expecting Bindiya's ears to be whacked. Deven was actually too shocked to react to his daughter's temerity. He was transfixed to his place in fact.

But Bindiya went on relentlessly,

"Father....we need to talk to Shri Girdhari....for transport we need to … to clean up this village…we live in such pitiable conditions…..he has power…..talk to him to do something about the flies.." Bindiya babbled, her voice tingeing with incoherency because she was not used to addressing her father this way.

"*What?*" Deven thundered.

His voice cleaved into her words and silenced her effectively.

"*Speak to who?* Are you mad! I can never do that…he is my master….I will never go to him with petty complaints…." Deven's voice actually shook with a trace of fear just thinking that Bindiya may just rush out of the hut and complain to Shri Girdhari right there and then!

"But father……today Jhumri died….we ….!"

"Shut your mouth you ungrateful girl…you will stay in the 'kotari' till you come to your senses…. *Speak to Maalik indeed!*"

He jerked Bindiya up and pushed her into the store, tightly dragging the loose 'door' and closing the entrance. As the gap through, which some light came in closed, Bindiya stared into the darkness. Her heart felt it would burst with frustration.

After a while she could hear her mother ladling milk. The shuffle of her feet near the door made Bindiya hope she was coming to her. But her foot falls faded to the other side of the courtyard and Bindiya's hopes of being let out were dashed! Loud slurping/ plus murmurs of talk from Bapu and her brothers, made Bindiya angrier. "Ma did not give me milk!" OOOOO!" Bindiya's heart suffered.

The next morning Shanta quietly slid the door of the 'kotari' a little and squeezed in through the slit. Her heart smote seeing Bindiya curled up sleeping in a corner. Gently she sat next to her daughter and caressed her head. Bindiya sat up startled. "Hush…. hush!"

Shanta hugged Bindiya, still patting her head softly. Bindiya settled into her mother's embrace, whispering, "Mother I must talk to Shri Girdhari…if I can't …..force Bapu…mother you know…"

Horrified Shanta pushed her away and narrowing her eyes glowered irately at her daughter. "Shut up! You are now a danger…you will stop this nonsense NOW! HUMMMMPH" Shanta snorted, *"you or Bapu… talk to Maalik?* Are you crazy?"

"But why can't we talk to him? Has he ever punished any one or said no one can speak to him?"

Shanta was completely thrown by her simple question, blustered,

"I…I…er…we will be thrown out from here…no one speaks to Maalik.. I -don't know why…never speak to Malik is what we know…do you hear me!" Shanta took recourse in whimpering self pity all of a sudden, "oh Bindiya, why are you rebelling? Don't you care about us anymore?" Helpless tears flowed down Shanta's eyes. Bindiya's heart moved in guilt. She staggered up crying, "no mother don't…forgive me….no….I won't…I won't speak…Ma… don't cry!"

Bindiya came out of the 'kotari' and resumed her daily life. An uneasy calm remained though. Bindiya noticed her mother rubbed her ankle more, that made her feel guilty and she tried to be as normal as ever. Deven was cold and remote towards her. Shanta was kinder and she tried to make amends for his behaviour. There was a stressed subdued air around Bindiya. When her brothers wanted to play Bindiya brushed them off rudely. She would sit and stare into space most times. Her heart cried for her best friend Jhumri. When Bindiya shut her eyes the vision of Jhumri's lifeless body sprang up. It shook her heart. "They are filthy…never wash hands, dirty animal, stinky…..disease…..no hospitals…they die………she died poor thing…sob…Jhumri……." The teachers/ Chaya/Ammah-ji's/the neighbour's conversations tangoed in uneven beats through Bindiya's mind. Uncontrolled tears wet her cheeks and flowed unchecked. Seeing her parents she had to quickly hide her grief; they seemed not to understand at all.

Seven

The next morning, even before dawn broke, Phuliya, a neighbour's daughter called from the lane, "Shanta 'chachi,' (aunty)...Shanta chachi!"

"Phuliya...what happened? Shanta hurriedly went to the entrance.

"Namaste, greetings, chachi...we are going to pack wheat grains...we need one extra hand.. Can Bindiya be spared?"

"Of course...Bindiya...*Bindiya!*" Shanta shook her awake. Within ten minutes Bindiya joined the group making their way to the sheds. They would be paid five rupees and given one meal. Bindiya was relieved for this work. At least she was not thinking about Jhumri. Phuliya was older to her, but good fun.

Phuliya's face had a disfiguring one inch mark that ran down the top of her left cheek. It was a result of an infected boil that had erupted on her face when she was a child. Dayaji had dabbed the boil with little acid to burst it. The boil burst. But what it did also was to split open skin; spill a very tiny fraction and burn her cheek! No amount of fuller's earth or sandal wood pastes cooled the burn that now was badly infected and festering! Fortunately for Phuliya, her parents had to leave her with her mother's sister, or her aunt, to baby sit whilst they left for an arduous pilgrimage! The aunt lived in the district. She was horrified when she saw her baby niece suffering because of the wound. Immediately Phuliya was taken to a medical clinic some hours away. The absence of Phuliya's parents made this task easier. A local doctor took care of the infection and some ointments fixed the wound. Yet strangely for some unexplainable reasons Phuliya or her parents never acknowledged this good work by the doctor. In fact they were very annoyed that Phuliya had been taken to a clinic! "The wound would have healed with Dayaji's medicines!" They kept insisting ignoring how healthy the wound looked. The ointments were stopped and the mark remained! For no cause she, Phuliya also liked to think the worst of doctors; her loyalties to Dayaji unshaken.

Presently chattering the group of six hiked ahead. Bindiya's heart started with sorrow when she chanced to see 'Laxmi' the cow grazing in a meadow. Her mind diverted to Jhumri. Biting her under lip she pushed back her tears.

"Come on come on we don't have all day….!" One of the employed help from the mansion supervising the proceedings shouted.

"Here this is your pile….!" Bindiya was handed a 'sup,' a one side open flat basket specifically made to clean wheat, pulses, cereals etc. Sighing Bindiya sat. Digging the open side of into the pile of wheat Bindiya managed to lift off the right amount. "Jhak jhak" she threw up the wheat grains and with practised expertise she winnowed the grain separating the wheat from the chaff!

Though the grain had already been threshed these manual measures were still taken. Bindiya and the others would then help fill sacks with the cleaned grain.

Already, four men were rapidly filling wheat into sacks. Two bullock carts stood outside the shed. The sacks of wheat would be transported to the grain 'mandi,' market, in them. Sometimes a 'jugaar' was used or even a tempo to transport wheat sacks.

The shed was hot and Bindiya could feel her body dampen with perspiration. But the money was precious. Phuliya sitting next to her was muttering, "My mother is unwell......she is vomiting.....I must finish fast and go. Dayaji is coming to see her"

Bindiya coughed and tried to clear her throat. The dust and wheat husk tickled her throat. She finally managed to say,

"Dayaji? No he is not the right person...Take her to the hospital...." Bindiya purposely stared at her cheek.

Phuliya self consciously turned, so her cheek was hidden, to say,

"Hospital? A hospital means visiting government clinic in the district, which is two hours away and again a government hospital, which is another five hours away at the main city. That far away? Bah! My mother says there are male doctors....plus she firmly believes doctors are descendants of the 'asura's,' demons,...she will never go there."

"Dayaji is also male?" Bindiya retaliated, a little apprehensive to bring up the "cheek" issue directly.

Phuliya lowered her eyes and shrugged, "but we know him... my mother will never be comfortable with strange doctors, at even stranger hospitals."

"But why do they think like that? I have heard hospitals are places where you go to get cured."

"OOF so many questions...I have no answers. Let me work...I have to return home fast." Phuliya impatiently moved the "sup" faster.

Bindiya was effectively quietened. After that they worked in silence.

High noon work was stopped. "I am out of here" Phuliya informed Bindiya hastily jumping up and dusting her clothes.

A mid-day meal was served. Bindiya uninterestedly ate her food and returned to the next pile assigned to her. Phuliya took half wage and rushed away. The supervisor came to Bindiya, "finish her work also I will pay you her half too!"

Bindiya head bent, just nodded.

They were at the sheds till dusk. Finally they collected their wages and treaded back home. Bindiya sniffed, and snorted. The husk tickled her nose. She coughed to clear her throat. She felt quite exhausted and tetchy.

Even though she had earned more than she had bargained for Bindiya felt no joy; since her mind revolved around Jhumri all times.

When she tiredly reached home the first sounds she heard was that of someone retching.

Eight

It was her brother Montu. The sounds of his retching clearly heard.

"Dayaji will here soon.. one dose of his bitter medicine and you will be fine. Bapu sent him a word…he is busy…many others in the surrounding areas are afflicted with, vomiting and upset tummies too…but he is coming then my son you shall be fine." Shanta, pulled her sari veil nearer her forehead and patted Montu as he retched into the drain. Holding her son Shanta led him back into the hut. Bindiya watched them horrified. Seething she followed her mother in.

"Hush Montu baba, Dayaji will be here…" Shanta cajoled as she helped Montu lie on his mat outside in the inner courtyard. Montu moaned and closed his eyes, his bile obviously rising again.

Bindiya could hardly get the words out, spitting and stammering,

"DAYAJI… .THAT KILLER…….never…I wont let him touch Montu……take him to the hospital…his condition has just started…..please before it is too late…Ma! Jhumri died because of this sickness….what is wrong with you? He will kill Montu too…."

"Quiet….how dare you bring those words out….Montu will not die…you wretched girl—you use death and Montu's name in the same breath?" Shanta quickly closed her eyes asked for forgiveness looking skywards.

Overcome by fuming anger, Shanta scrambled up and shook Bindiya, "Silence…don't you dare speak about Dayaji like that…."

"Ma please…please ….!"

"Shanta Bhabhiji!" Dayaji called from the door.

Shanta wildly turned her face towards the direction the voice had called from.

"I will tell him to get out….no Ma…no!" "NEVER…YOU RUDE GIRL!"

It took Shanta all her strength to push Bindiya into the Kotari and slide the door. The door was heavy and if it fell it would directly hit Montu stretched in the inner courtyard. Bindiya knew she from the inside could not slide or open the 'kotari' without risking the door falling down and injuring Montu. With the heavy feeling that she was not going to be heard Bindiya sagged down on to the floor; she held her head and sobbed helplessly. Soon her tears dried up too.

"Oh no he has soiled his knickers again….Dayaji it is not stopping.. he vomits then purges…!"

Shanta's low voice filtered through the door, Bindiya bit her lip and strained her ears to catch the conversations. Dayaji murmured something that Bindiya could not make out what. Anger rose like a black cloud in her innards; Bindiya felt like tearing the door down and barging into the courtyard. But she did not do that. Bindiya still held on to some hope she could convince her mother to let her get real help for Montu. Patiently Bindiya waited.

After at least an hour Shanta pushed the door and cautiously looked at her daughter. Bindiya seemed calmer.

"If you are going to behave you can come out." Shanta worded unsympathetically.

Bindiya swallowed. Her mother's face was set. Bindiya slowly grasped that her mother was not going to come around or listen; holding these heavy thoughts in her heart, Bindiya made her way out as Shanta stood aside.

Dayaji had left. But the stink of his burning herbs and roots assailed her nose.

"Montu….." Bindiya fell to the floor next to her brother and caressed his cold forehead.

Montu turned and looked at her. He moaned and rolled his eyes. His face was ashen.

A groan interrupted them. It was Bontu.

"Ma…aaaah….Ma!" Bontu called from the door.

"What? Bontu what happened?" Bindiya asked her obviously miserable brother.

"Didi…aaaah my stomach hurts…I am feeling sick…!"

Bindiya's heart sank, she looked at Bontu with dismay then returned her gaze to Montu lying thin and pale.

Suddenly Jhumri's pale face flashed into her mind. "No!" Bindiya fiercely whispered. She sprang up and darted outside; almost pushing Bontu aside.

"Didi…whaaaaa!"

Rudely pushing Bontu aside, Bindiya scuttled down the lane and reached the banyan tree. The men folk were sitting and talking around the tree. Her father was there too. Between them was the oldest member of the lane. He was highly respected. Bindiya ran up to him and in a loud voice said, " Shayam Taya, elder uncle, listen to me!"

There was a stunned silence. Not waiting Bindiya blurted in a desperate pleading voice, "Please 'Taya' we need to get Montu to a hospital…now Bontu is also complaining. Oh dear. Dayaji is incapable of handling this sickness….please…help me get Montu to the hospi…..!"

"WHACK!"

Her father came up behind and cuffed her on the head, "get out of here!" he hissed.

Bindiya, ignoring the numbing pain, pushed him away screaming, "Bapu listen…Montu will die….do something!"

There was a collective gasp; Bindiya did not care, she went on relentlessly, "Bapu be sensible…Shri Girdhari is a kind man ask him to provide transport…do something *Montu is going die otherwise!*"

"Stop this nonsense girl!" Shayam Taya thundered. Bindiya stopped midway with her mouth still open. Turning to Deven, Shayam sneered with sarcasm, "why Devenji ? Can't you control a mere girl? She spells trouble for the village….she plans to talk to Maalikji and bring shame to our village….she insults the esteemed Dayaji..if she was my daughter I would take care that she never has the boldness to speak thus in public!" With that Shayam Tau derisively turned his back. He was joined by the others; Bindiya and her father efficiently cut off from any further communication in that small space. "Shayamji I…!"

Deven defensively started to say, but the company had turned their back to him. *No one was listening to Deven*. His shame was complete.

With an angry roar, Deven grabbed Bindiya's arm and pulled her.

"No Bapu no….Bapu *listen*…!" Bindiya tried to dig her heels in and resisted. But Deven naturally was stronger.

Enraged Deven hauled her home. Inside the hut he flung her down, in one swift angry movement he extricated a stout half burnt stick from under the stove.

Aghast, Bindiya covered her face and twisted on her stomach, the blows poured relentlessly on her upper and lower back.

Bindiya could not feel the pain after some time. In blind fury Deven beat her single-mindedly yelling, "you rebel…you obstinate rebel…I know how to take care of rebels like you!"

Shanta, Bontu cried and begged him to stop but his temper was far gone. It took Bontu and Shanta's combined strength to drive him away. All this time sick Montu pale and shivering, sat up slightly, balanced on one elbow blinked and stared at them!

"Throw her into the Kotari!" Deven scathingly spat, still panting from the fury his emotions had put him into.

In-spite of the commotion the recent activities invited, Shanta somehow managed to tug Bindiya to the "kotari". Shaking and disbelieving that her father had actually spanked her, Bindiya still feebly resisted,

"OH…OH…No Bapu….oh!"

She was shoved in and the door was dragged and pressed against the entrance, effectively shutting her within. "Montu… Jhumri…die….hospital!"

Words in a jumble forced her to ignore the lacerating pain her back as she struggled up. She cautiously pressed her head to the door. Montu's whimpers came clearly through. He was sleeping right next to the door.

Later, through her miserable state, Bindiya fathomed that Bapu was leaving for cattle duty to the sheds. It was his turn with another tiller to take charge of the cattle for the next week. He had to report to duty at night.

The cattle sheds were built away from their village. In rotation, two tillers were given cattle duty and whosoever was on duty, collected the cattle before dawn and brought them out to graze/ then depute to, the buffaloes, to whosoever, to work in the fields etc; at dusk, the same tillers on duty had to guide the herd and leave them at the sheds. Four supervisors, employed by the landlord, did the accounting for the cattle at the shed.

"I have to do something….Bapu is so clouded by his own beliefs he will never change…Montu has to be saved! Bontu too is going to be sick…."

I cannot open this door..*Montu is sleeping there, he may get hurt*…I need to escape…but how??"

Defiance was not a characteristic encouraged by anyone in this village especially from girls. But Bindiya after her one life changing experience of a visit to the Mansion was infused by rebellion. Jhumri dying fuelled it even more. Her mind now worked out a means to escape the "kotari".

No broken bones and spanking pain fading, Bindiya verified this comment by rubbing her back and straightening up.

With a once all over look, Bindiya checked the kotari. "I got it!" her foot rubbed the spool of moon light patterned on the rough floor, pouring from a hole in the thatched roof on top. The hole was to be repaired before the rains. I have to escape. With all her might she hauled up the sacks of farm implements, coal, wood and straw. Panting she directly pulled them under the hole in the roof. 'UMGHHH!" Disappointed Bindiya realised the sacks still did not reach the roof. Missing it by some inches, even if she stretched she could not reach the outlet. She knew if she pushed the door Ma would be awake, moreover she could not risk injuring Montu who she thought was sleeping right outside the door! . Bindiya looked around. Her heart gave a happy thump. Two iron pails and one tiny drum lay in the kotari too. She was thankful for the moon light! Quietly putting the drum first then the pails one on top of the other, Bindiya taking advantage of her small frame, ginger stepped up. Balancing on the uneven sacks/ drum/ pails, she stretched her hands to reach the wooded beams of the roof. Still not reaching, with high risk of falling from her shaking perch, Bindiya sprung up and in split seconds caught the wooden frame on which the thatch lay.

"Trnnnujkk bang dummm!" the pail and the drum rolled off the sacks. Bindiya was hanging in the middle of the "kotari" roof! Alarmed because she was sure the noise would wake the neighbourhood up, Bindiya, suspended like an askew pendulum, waited. She could hear her own uneven breath playing panicked pin pong; alertly her ears concentrated hard into the silence to gauge whether she had awoken any one. Luckily no one came. Relieved Bindiya proceeded to escape.

Wondering if the beam would give way, Bindiya pushed upwards. "Unggggh" she managed to push her head through the hole. With all her might Bindiya pushed and thrust her whole body out, and slithered on to the hay surface of the roof! Fresh air assailed her nostrils. Triumphantly Bindiya with full efforts propelled upwards and out. Slowly Bindiya stood up meaning to see where she could jump off and reach down below.

"AAAAAAAAAAAAAAHHHHHHHHH!"

The roof was not strong enough and with the pandemonium aided by her scream, breaking wood beam, hay and roof stuffing, she rocketed down! Yes. Bindiya fell through the roof; into the next room where her mother and brother were sleeping; "AAAAAAAH- DHUMMMMMMBBBBBBBB!" *She landed on to Bapu's empty bed!*

"Thwackkkkkk!" rope and wood cracked! "Whaaaa"

"Aieeeeee"

"Ma"

"Ummmmm"

These were individual reactions of every occupant of the room!

Montu too was inside, Bindiya noticed even as she struggled to get off her father's cot. No one was expecting Bindiya to fall out of the roof so there was confusion. Not waiting to give explanations Bindiya pushed out of the bed and bolted out of the hut!

"Stop….stop…..help!" Shanta cried. Not sure what was happening.

The uproar had the dogs barking maniaclly, but Bindiya just ran.

Bindiya sprinted so fast that by the time her family realised what had happened she was far away from the hut and the village!

Peering into the moon lit outdoors Bindiya stopped to breathe. She bent low, holding her knees and gasped for breath.

Behind her she heard shouts, laced with barks. Not waiting, Bindiya sprinted forward even faster. Her panicky and frightened wits not really able to assemble clarity of judgment, hazily directed her to the main highway.

After a while when Bindiya was sure she was not being followed she halted. Bindiya thought her heart would burst; she took deep breaths. One random thought actually wavered and told her to stop. Shaking loose from the notion, Bindiya muttered to herself, "No, I cannot give up! Bolstering her tired mind and body Bindiya began to walk. She tried as best to remain within the shadows. She knew it was not safe to be out at this time, but Bindiya was driven. Bindiya recognised the shadowy mango orchards on the side of the road. She doggedly trudged ahead till with relief she recognised the grain sheds. If she kept walking she would reach the 'bada' road,high way, from there straight road leads me to the "Haveli"!

Bindiya tried to recall the routes she had taken when she had come with her father to the Haveli.

Bindiya must have walked for at least two hours when she arrived at the cattle sheds…..."from here (left) comes the highway", she mumbled.. Bindiya plodded on. When she reached the apron of the sheds she froze. In front of her stood her father!

Yes, Bapu and his comrade were talking right on the square strip in front of the sheds. *Oh no Bapu is on cattle duty…he is here…I have to hide!*

Thankfully he did not see her and taking this advantage Bindiya, promptly withdrawing into the grove of shadowy trees, waited.

"Grrrrrrrr"

Bindiya's eyes widened and her blood raced. Sweat trailed dots all over her upper lip. Slowly she traced the growl and gasped.

A black mongrel dog ominously crouched at the entry of the

tree belt, balefully stared at her, baring its teeth!

"Sssssh"

Ignoring her—the dog warningly growled and came closer and closer till he positioned himself right at her feet!

"Shssssh!" Bindiya hushed the dangerous looking animal whose wild shining eyes had no compromise in them.

"GRRRRRR"

"Moti....koeeee!" someone called whistling.

Bindiya backed into a tree and the dog barked full throated now, pawing the ground and exposing its teeth.

"Moti!" Came the call again

This somehow encouraged the dog and in an outburst he yowled in a series of sharp panic-stricken barks!

"Moti....tooeeeey! (whistle)."

The permanent cattle shed employee called Jeetu, ambled towards the trees calling Moti.

"Jeetu....why is Moti barking like that?" Bindiya heard Bapu inquire.

Even as Jeetu walked up, Bindiya with a sinking heart saw her father walking along *with him, to check too!* Apparently there were just two of them present and of course Moti! The rest would come early in the morning to take charge from Deven, who was on a watchman duty with Jeetu.

Moti by now had turned frenzied. Bindiya clasped the tree trunk, her back pressing against it hard, drawing up her knees and proactively prepared to dodge any bites when they came! Her fear flooded brain synchronising with the continuous barking.

I am going to be caught...Bapu is going to kill me! Bindiya's heart quaked as she acknowledged the fact that she was *cornered.*

Nine

"Tweeetoooey- Moteee…..what?" Jeetu bend and tousled Moti's short furred head.

Seeing his master, Moti stopped barking and whined; concurrently, albeit eagerly running to the tree and back to Jeetu.

"What is he saying?" Bapu following closely asked.

"I don't know…even a bird can set this dog into endless hysteria. The other day a goat was loose and Moti almost died barking." Chuckled Jeetu, "well I see nothing here…hmmm!" Jeetu stood right under the tree peering upwards. Jeetu was not to blame if he spotted nothing! The tricky shadows of dim darkness pouring flashes of changeling light from the moon hardly gave him good "seeing" sight!

Moti had passed hysterics and now was verging on mad chokinghe lost his bark you see and was choking and trying to woof!

Where was Bindiya?

Right atop the tall tree; in split seconds she managed a clumsy 'ulat,' the backwards flip, and like a nimble monkey had managed to climb the leafiest, darkest part of the tree and held still. She was not breathing. Elongated like a leopard on a branch, Bindiya waited. Her elbows burned, "I must have grazed them!"

"Nothing Moti—come onnnnn ugggghhhh!" Floated up a gruff voice of Jeetu urgently yanking his dog by the fur of its neck!

But Moti refused to budge. He dug his paws in and resisted completely to be hauled away. Bindiya thought she would suffer a heart failure. "Drat..Moti scat!" Bindiya wished the dog away.

After a few tense seconds in which; in response to Moti's hoarse choky barks; Bapu and Jeetu stood by the tree looking here and there, Jeetu grabbed Moti by the neck and dragged him. Moti struggled and broke free. Irritated Jeetu tightened his hold asking Bapu to hand him the collar and chain. The chain was a thick links of iron and the collar a studded one. When visitors came to visit Moti was tied with it. Bapu hurriedly complied. Collared and chained Moti was lugged away. Bindiya did not dare to move. Within five minutes, when Moti was unchained at the shed, he came bounding back.

"Something is on that tree!" Jeetu who had panted up with Bapu following closely uttered. Sweat broke out on Bindiya's forehead.

"I can't see anything…it is too dark…hmmm….ooooey any one there…come out!" Bapu sternly bellowed. That had Moti croak once more with a hoarse "yip yip".

Bindiya dug her body more into the branch.

"I think I will climb up and check; let me get a torch! Make a perfunctory, token, check at least" Jeetu muttered peering into the tall heavily branched and shadowed tree.

Bapu bend and held Moti. Bindiya felt her body shake with fear. Jeetu returned and grasping the torch in his teeth he prepared to climb. "Careful could be a snake up there!" Bapu warned.

"Snake?" Jeetu hesitated.

Some cosmic good fortune was relaying its protectiveness for Bindiya at that very moment!

The investigations were rudely disrupted when with a ferocious growl-ly whine. Moti unexpectedly shook loose from Bapu's grasp and with a croaky yip chased something?!?!?

"Meowwwwww grawllllln"

"Yip yip-wooofff—growl-- cough!" Moti was off, into the tree belt, like a bullet choking and croaking since his earlier high-pitched barks had totally blocked his throat!!

What had fallen out from the tree?

Moti came bounding back chasing a...*Cat!*

A Cat, hackles risen, desperately shot out from the shadows and roiled between the legs of the two men before running high speed ahead!

"Arrrey(oh) a cat.....sigh....a cat is troubling Moti!" Jeetu's explanatory voice tore the air over the din.

Bapu too heaved a relieved sigh.

Yes, little Miss Cat was sneaking from the tree belt to get to the milk drums. She had nothing to do with the goings on under the particular tree, which was garnering so much of attention then! She just happened to be stealing directed by a very hungry stomach. Moti would have none of that. Breaching her private scrounge for food, he tracked her wildly, thus rendering her into a befuddled panicked state, egging her to *run!* Leading to the assumption by Jeetu and Bapu that she had fallen down from the very tree they were under! Actually fear from a savagely annoyed chasing Moti, had meandered her paths towards them!

"OOOOOey, (whistle), come here Moti!"

They left in a commotion of shouts trying to control the dog. Bindiya expelled a long breath!

Soon there was absolute silence. 'I guess they have caught the errant Moti' Bindiya decided. Waiting to be very sure Bindiya softly dropped from the tree.

"Oh please don't let Moti come again....Bindiya prayed.

Peering into the darkness, Bindiya espied the sheds, which were two hundred metres away. To get to the roads she needed to cross the sheds. Bindiya stopped and cautiously glanced around.

The place was deserted, though she could hear the buffaloes grunting and mildly moving. Sneaking in a very stealthy way in the semi darkness, she tip-toed across the shed; darting between the haystacks swiftly; it was an open area and Bindiya was terrified of being caught!

"Mooo....grwoooon!!" Buffaloes bellowed softly. Feeling that any moment she would be nabbed Bindiya bunched her body, bent double and hurried her steps.

What Bindiya did not know that her father and Jeetu were sleeping at the open cemented area at the back, from where she was!

Unaware, sure that Bapu and Jeetu plus Moti were sleeping elsewhere, Bindiya halted and accustomed her eyes to the moonlit path.

Then it happened.

Bindiya unthinkingly stood by the side of the sheds. When she turned left at a little distance, with a sinking heart, she noticed two beds, two sleeping men, her father and Jeetu.

The barometers of her shock and reaction forked crazily upwards when Moti, furious and wanting vindications, with a mighty roar drove towards her out of the blue from under Jeetu's cot!!

There was a problem for Moti though. He could not reach her. One she was not so close, two *he was tied to Jeetu's bed!*

Moti had been chained to one of the bed leg of Jeetu's bed; his continuous restlessness had inspired his being tied up! \

Earlier Moti sniffed into the air. Something was happening in front. Hmmm what? Tense and alert, he had raised his nose under the cot and sniffed a low growl grazing his throat; now seeing Bindiya all hell broke loose!

"WWWarkkkkkkkkkkkkkkkkkkkkkkkkkkkkkkkkkkkkk!" Moti lunged, Jeetu, just moments ago sailing in sleep land is rudely shaken awake and given an unscheduled ride! Eyes rolling Jeetu jack-knifed to sitting position, clutching the sides of the cot! "Whoaaaaaaaa!" The cot and its unwilling passenger hampered Moti and bedlam ensued! Bindiya did not wait to see anything she just ran!

"AAARGH….OW…BAM/…….DHAM…WOOOF   YIP GROWL….AAARGH!" Mixed renditions strung the space, cleaving brutally through the otherwise tranquil sleepy time zones, like scratchy music from a bad violin player!

But this was all happening behind Bindiya! Oh no! She was not stopping!

Bindiya sprinted ahead so fast giving the impression that she was being chased by a hundred tigers!

After walking probably for hours Bindiya slouched against a tree stump and rested. She squinted into the night and gauged directions. She closed her eyes and heard the nocturnal sounds! The tree inhabitants: birds flurried about, squirrels chipped, crickets trilled, relaxing her. To aid her restful pose a slight gust grazed her neck, cooling her.

"Water….water…!" Bindiya hummed under her breath. Her throat was burning with thirst.

"I cannot be here, *I must move*!" A voice in her mind urged Bindiya effectively vetoing the idea of looking for water.

Sluggishly, Bindiya rose and thought, "cannot have water too… will have to keep walking."

Her trails turned from grassy routes to the road tracks.

She stealthily crossed parked trucks silently shadowed against the skyline. Some places she even saw the drivers and cleaners of the trucks sleeping under their vehicles!

It must have been half and hour of trek when Bindiya had the most beautiful sound in her ears. The sound of water! "*tip-tap, tip-tap-gurgle-tip-tap*!" Up ahead in the darkness she made out a cemented square and a tap. The tap was leaking so someone had placed a bucket under it. Lifting the almost full bucket Bindiya drenched herself from head to toe. "AAAH" the wash refreshed her. Licking the droplets off her mouth and chin, she opened the tap, "grunsplassssshhhhh", as water gushed forth Bindiya drank to her hearts content!

"pownnnnnnnnnnnnnnnnnnnnnnnnnnnnn!"

When the truck bore down on her from behind she never realised. She had been walking for hours; the first strains of light were spreading in the sky. The shriek of brakes and blaring horn scared her to jump aside only to fall badly into an unmarked ditch dug out at the side of the road. The truck rumbled off but Bindiya lay still. Exhaustion over came her; softly sleep lapped her lids. She just could not lift herself up from the ditch. Sleep.......slowly overcame her senses and soon she was lost to the world.

"Is she dead?"

"Hmmm....looks like it..."

Voices sliced through her sleep numbed her brain and Bindiya forced her eyelids to open.

The ring of concerned faces staring down at her startled her and she sprung up to realise she still was in the ditch and it was bright morning. Traffic on the highway was gaining momentum. Trucks cars, tempo's, other vehicles whizzed past noisily. A few pedestrians and cyclists curious to see a girl lying unconscious in the ditch had stopped to wonder.

Swallowing and licking her lips to press down the nervousness that threatened to swamp her Bindiya tried to stand. But she toppled down.

"Whoa...girl....what is the matter? I think she is mad...she looks crazy.... stay away!" Someone said in a voice traced with hysteria.

"I- am alright...let me go "

"Where are we stopping you?.. Go...right away for all we care" Some one else in the crowd rudely intoned. His words had the crowd disperse and Bindiya found herself alone.

It dawned on Bindiya that she was actually inside a big puddle and not a ditch. Struggling up Bindiya disgustedly realised her clothes were muddy and wet, her hair coated too. Rubbing her arms and straightening her clothes Bindiya blinked and surveyed where she was…Her eyes wandered to the opposite side; further away; she saw the place where she so desperately wanted to go to: Shri Girdhari's "Haveli"!

Bindiya even in the darkness had not gone wrong on her bearings! Celebrating this feeling Bindiya rejoiced exultantedly!

Over undulating fields across the road the white wall and the parapets of the Havelli could be seen at a distance. She recognised the wall and the doors that sparkled blue!

The biggest challenge of her journey now presented itself. How was she going to cross over to the other side? *The highway was buzzing with fast vehicles!* Bindiya had never crossed a road let alone a busy highway. Positioning herself at the edge of the path her heart sank, the horn blowing whizzing contraptions mercilessly rode down not waiting or giving a pass even for a split second. What was Bindiya going to do…her destination right in front of her yet it seemed so far!

Ten

Bindiya tried to step on the road to cross over but "powwwnwwwnwwn!" a horn would blare and a sweep of vehicles would tear down the road giving Bindiya just seconds to spring backwards and freeze in fear! "How will I cross?"

"Bow bow!" Bindiya glanced sideways and with amusement noticed a dog, a mongrel standing right besides her. The mongrel was calling out to another mongrel—that was standing across the road!

"Is he your friend?" Bindiya asked her words edged with a smile.

Ignoring her, the dog continued to bark.

'Hmmm you are as helpless as I am…hey hey…!"

Bindiya nervously watched as the dog stepped away from her. He moved on to the road.

Umm, what is he doing? I wonder? Bindiya gnawed her lower lip anxiously.

The mongrel looked left then right, gauged the distance of the oncoming vehicles and ran…..in fact like a shot bolted across. Even as a succession of vehicles came bearing down he was over to the other side meeting his pal!!

"Oh……he is smart……Thanks doggy…I guess that the way you do it." Bindiya grinned.

Here goes, Bindiya took a deep breath and watched the traffic coming from the left then right. As soon as she saw a minuscule of a seconds gap she sprinted so fast that even when she reached she kept running only stopping when she was in the middle of the fields!

"Ha ha ha ha!" I did it!" Her heart rejoiced. Getting her breath back she stared ahead at the looming edifice of the 'havelli' in front.

It took Bindiya another fifteen minutes to traipse across the field. Finally she reached the white wall. She noticed that a car stood by the open blue doors.

Even as she was walking up she saw Shri Girdhari's wife who Billu had called 'Madamji' stepped out of the car, she was followed by Chaya.

With an exultant yelp thoughtlessly Bindiya ran to them garbling, "help…Montu will die….Bontu……Jhumri……oh…… namaste, listen!" Bindiya after her travails uncorked her emotions to flow unhindered like the fizz out of a soda drink! In her energised nervousness she stuttered and words tripped forward disjointedly! The arrival of a dishevelled, crazily muttering girl did not do much for 'Madame-ji's' nerves. One can safely assume that for her daughter Chaya too!

There was a chaos.

Madame-ji screamed, Chaya screamed, the guards screamed, but most of all, distraught Bindiya trying to get her words across, screamed!

The grand finale of the situation came to a close, when in one distracted movement Bindiya caught hold of "Madame-ji's" hand desperately to get her attention!

"Eeeks…she is attacking Mummy…..get her away!" Chaya protested in a terrified way.

"Guards, driver, what nonsense, what is this?" "Madam-ji" shouted pushing Bindiya so hard she knocked her down.

"Ummmmmf!" Finding this to be opportunity, Bindiya was dragged away by four hands simultaneously.

"B-ut...*listen*! Leave me...let me go..I have to tell her....." Bindiya dug her heels and tried to resist desperately. She failed since the strength of four guards proved stronger!

Not even looking at her 'Madam-ji' was furiously scolding the men guarding the doors, "how dare this scrap of filth manage to touch me; charge on me like this...are you people blind....?"

The guards cowered and bend their heads low.

"See what the beggar wants, feed her and send her off! 'Madamji' arrogantly dismissed.

Chaya who was jammed in a defensive pose against the car shouted "call the police...lock her up...oh!"

"Hush Chaya....come, come calm down...it is just a beggar.... come, come!"

"Madamji" consoled Chaya and led her through the doors.

As soon as they left, the guards turned menacingly to Bindiya. One of them charged at her boxed her hard over the ears. Bindiya went sprawling down again.

"You beggar girl, see what you did you embarrassed us in front of Madame."

The cuff on the head enraged Bindiya so much that she sprung up and with one kick she sent one guard flying. The other three were so shocked that they were immobilised for a few seconds. Taking advantage Bindiya bolted like a young unbridled horse after 'Madam-ji' through the blue doors.

Chaya and her mother were near the kitchens when Bindiya caught up with them. Bindiya screamed, "Listen to me....*please.*"

"Mummy she followed us waaaaa help Mummmyyyyyy!" Chaya sacredly holding her mother blubbered!

But before any one could react, the guards caught Bindiya

and tried to lug her away. "Please listen…please listen!" Bindiya resisted

"Stop….stop…you are hurting the girl…leave her alone! At least listen to what she has to say…." A voice commanded in the melee.

Eleven

It was 'Teacherji.' Along with the cooks, Ammah-ji they had run out too see what the commotion was all about.

"Didi,   (sister), Chaya, you go inside...I will handle this." "Teacherji" said.

"Tanya ...don't get involved, let them handle her." Madame-ji said.

"Didi go." "Teacherji" or Tanya firmly said.

Shrugging they left; even the help and the cooks followed them in. Only Ammah-ji, the guards, Bindiya and Tanya were left.

"Guards leave her." With a reluctant air the guards unhanded her and walked away.

"Now girl, what is the matter?' Tanya looked at Bindiya and asked.

"I-t is -m-me?" Bindiya said hesitantly.

"Do I know you?" Tanya quizzed through her glasses in a puzzled way.

"G-Bindiya...B-apu—er Deven...er..is m-y father!" Bindiya stammered.

"Who?"

"Bindiya...Bapu—er Deven...er..is m-y father!" Bindiya

repeated a little louder frantically.

"Oh- my -gosh! She is the slum waif who came the other day. Deven's daughter...what is wrong with her...she is even dirtier than last time..look at her soaked in dried mud....!"

"Hush Ammah-ji....Bindiya...hhhm yes I remember....ok... why did you scare my sister and niece like that?"

"Y-ou said..wash hands..Montu....!" Slowly Bindiya related why she was behaving so crazily. First she jumbled up the events—but Tanya softly and gently got the whole story out.

Twelve

The ambulance could not reach Deven's hut because there was no road. But the para medics along with Tanya and Bindiya went straight to the hut walking.

"Why is there a crowd outside my house?!" Bindiya gasped. "The worst has happened... Montu...oh no!"

Increasing her pace Bindiya ran as fast as she could. Tanya who was gingerly trying to walk through the unpaved lane and ignore the stench of the drain tried to hurry too. When Bindiya burst into the hut, she froze with horror.

Shanta crouched besides, Montu who was spread eagled on the floor. She was wailing. Deven, Bontu, Dayaji and another neighbour stood aside in mute silence.

Aparently Sunheri, Jhumri's mother was back. She stood with her children there too. Her husband was with Deven.

"Ma...Montu....what...!" Bindiya rushed in.

"Bindiya? Oh Bindiya...Bindiya he does not speak.....oh Bindiya!" Shanta seeing her daughter wailed louder. Shanta did not know whether to be relieved to see the return of her errant daughter or cry for her apparently dying son.

Deven, though relieved to see Bindiya, did not show it. He

glowered at her. He had spent a hellish dawn, when returning from duty; handling her disappearance and his son's illness.

Before Bindiya could react, the paramedics rushed in.

"Keep aside....let them check the child!" Tanya too stepped in saying. A visibly affected company stepped aside to allow 'choti, (younger) madam' in.

"There is a pulse...hurry....get him to the ambulance...the child is dehydrated needs a drip!" one paramedic pronounced. Within minutes the stretcher came and Montu was lifted up. Meanwhile another paramedic checked Bontu too and advised him to accompany them to the hospital as well. As Montu was being rushed out a small voice asked, "M-y mother...er...my mother!" It was Phuliya. She looked harassed and tired the mark on her cheek prominent. Bindiya understood what she was trying to say. "Tanya didi please, her mother too suffers....can she go to the hospital also?"

"Of course...which is your hut?"

Tanya made the medics understand the directions.

Tanya grimaced and addressed the onlookers, "listen please anytime you have the same symptoms please don't take herbs etc. Go to a proper doctor. In the meanwhile just make a bottle of boiled and cooled water in which a clean teaspoon of salt and a teaspoon of sugar has been dissolved...... to be taken in sips..... you need...." Her attention turned to someone and she stopped talking. She was staring at Chotu, Jhumri's brother. "This child has jaundice...I know I have seen all this before...are you alright boy?" Tanya addressed a very weak looking embarrassed boy.

Chotu did not answer.

Sunheri protectively stood besides her son. "Are you his mother?"

Swallowing Sunhri nodded.

"Please take him to the doctors...he can die if he does not get help! Oh no!" Tanya exclaimed, "even this one looks jaundiced…..” she said looking at an urchin standing nearby. His mother too immediately came, fussing with her head cover, to stand beside her son, glaring balefully under her veil! Sunheri resolutely stood, with no intentions of listening. This inter change was interrupted by,

“Where are they taking my son….where?” Shanta broke in hysterically still not comfortable with her son being evacuated thus. She placed herself in front of the medics, blocking their way.

“Shanta Bhabhiji…let him go to the hospital…..he will be in good hands.”

This was one voice no one expected to hear! Daya-ji!

Yes, Dayaji with never seen humbleness coaxed Shanta to let her son go to the hospital. Dayaji seemed to be dealing with his own private hell with the passing away of Jhumri. Seeing the business-like efficiency of the medic's he decided to swallow his ego and go with the flow!

A collective hush gripped them all. Dayaji's features mapping mixed expressions, denoting resignation and sheepishness, nodded, as Shanta open mouthed stared at him. Reluctantly Shanta moved aside.

Dayaji looked at Sunheri and the other lady. Sunheri seemed to give up.

In this surprised hush the medics began to leave with their patients. Sunheri looked back and then called her older son, “go with them.” He complied immediately.

Tanya looked at the company and clicked her tongue, “what is this, dysentery, jaundice? Appaling….you apparently are not starving and food is in abundance, by what Bindiya told me! This is not the case everywhere—you are lucky! But you are harbouring illness because you maintain such unhygienic standards! Please change your ways—you are promoting an epidemic-type disaster by not going to the hospital.”

"Go to the hospital…..So far?" someone muttered.

Tanya stopped her pour of words and gnawed her under lip, slightly abashed, since she really had no answer why the hospital was so far. In this awkward silence, Deven, with a mutter to excuse him, coldly bypassed his daughter and followed the stretcher bearing medics.

Bindiya flushed at his coldness.

Tanya stepped out of the hut. At that point she took a hard look around her; to really see the surroundings. She took in the meshed with wires electric pole, blackened fire damaged huts, the drain, filthy garbage and random living conditions; scared, hesitant dwellers. She fully understood what Bindiya had been telling her. Her heart filled with sadness only to be replaced with a cry that said, "This all needs to change!" Tanya returned inside. The curious onlookers silently watched her. "Bindiya…Bindiya!" Shanta called infringing the moment, her arms spread out. Bindiya ran and hugged her mother. Bontu also joined the huddle. "My children, (sob)…..oh my children (sob)…...Montu-uuu," She

wailed stretch his name as if it would help clear the pain she felt in her heart! "Poor me…this is all beyond poor me…!" Shanta rocked and wailed in self pity and grief. "Shanta!"

This shout staunched the flooding river of words emitting from her mouth.

Deven had re-entered the hut, "Shanta come with me to the hospital. Sunheri Bhabhi will take care here. Bontu is also complaining so we have to show him to the doctor, so bring Bontu…er Bindiya too….come fast we will camp there till Montu is better. Chotu is also going with us. Rest are with Madame-ji's big doctor vehicle, ambulance. Satish has brought his 'Jugaar' we will get transport; we all can go…come."

"Wait!" Tanya interjected, "let me take Bindiya with me….I would really want her to come back home…Deven-ji…let her be with me till you are back." Tanya requested earnestly.

Deven hesitated. Even though his one son was being rushed to the hospital; his other son most likely examined by a doctor, Deven was still a little sceptical. He had to give in because Tanya madam had ordered it but his vibes were still remote and wintry towards this situation.

He was lucky that the other fellow tillers had offered to take over his work so he could deal with Montu's illness.

"Let her be with Bibiji, Madam!" Shanta interrupted, seemingly calmer.

Deven nodded, without looking at Bindiya he left. Shanta and Bontu hurriedly followed him.

"There is a reason I am taking you back Bindiya!" Tanya gurgled, cutely wrinkling her nose so her glasses propped up on her nose.

They were sitting in the back of a jeep heading back to the Havelli. Bindiya's parents and brothers had left for the hospital. Bindiya felt safe and secure with this kind 'didi,' sister as a mark of respect, and had no problems accompanying her. This 'didi' did not look down her nose and speak to her but actually treated her like a person!

"You my dear girl after a bath are going to talk to Shri Girdhari or Jeejaji, (brother in law)."

Bindiya's features creased perplexedly, bringing a spontaneous giggle from Tanya.

"Bindiya, Shri Girdhariji is married to my older sister, Kamna didi. Our parents live in Canada."

Tanya paused then explained into Bindiya's even more bewildered air, "Canada is a place far ,far away. It is a foreign land. Well, then what am I doing here—you want to know right?" Bindiya gulped and bounced her head agreeing.

"I am a part of a rural development group. Actually I teach slum children. But not here, I work with an NGO at another village. I am visiting my sister."

Bindiya was then given a detail on what was meant by NGO,

non government organization, and welfare activities done by her and her fellow social workers.

"We take help from the government even though we are not the government." Tanya clicked her tongue and explained what government meant before continuing, "we help the needy.... that is why we are called welfare groups...your village, imagine, is nowhere on our radar! You folks have actually insulated and isolated yourselves. No demands....nothing!"

"Didi Montu and Bontu the others, they will be fine....?" Bindiya going slightly off track asked.

"Yes mostly if medical help is on time, all is well!" Tanya assured her.

"Didi why is everyone sick?"

"Bad hygiene, bad water, all the things...that dirty drain.... mosquitoes, first it will be dysentery, then malaria then god knows what!"

Then with patient detail Bindiya was given a graphic description of the diseases her village was probably endangered with if they did not clean up fast! Later there was a comfortable silence as Bindiya mulled over what Tanya had told her.

"Er Chaya ...Beeji...you teach..." Bindiya timidly raised!

"Oh that Guru?'Teacherji' bit of Ammah-ji!" Tanya laughed outright before saying,

"Chaya studies in a hostel in America, again Tanya explained where America was. She is here for her summer vacations. I feel bad that she has no knowledge about our Indian systems, and is a total foreigner; so I keep tutoring her. Teasingly I have been re-christened '"Teacherji'!". Chaya is a good girl, but very spoilt being the only child. She takes everything including people for granted!" Tanya paused then said with a passionate glint in her eyes,

"You know Bindiya I love this country. I have been born and brought up abroad, but I cannot forget my roots. When Kamna didi got married and settled here I was very young. Fortunately

I began visiting India regularly. I even joined up a sociology course here, then took up a job with an NGO. We have such a rich and cultured heritage......!" Bindiya listened fascinated to Tanya. Suddenly, Bindiya loved being an Indian. She never knew beyond her village this country was an amazing fabric of enjoined cultures and ancient heritages! The family system and the warm interconnection of people she so took for granted was actually a social gift rather than a commonality anywhere else in the world.

In a little while Bindiya too was relating how she rebelled. After hearing her out Tanya commented,

"What hurts me is how we are allowing illiteracy and unawareness plus a lackadaisical, half hearted, attitude to ruin a very good thing. What does a village need? Awareness of healthy hygienic living, primary health centres, schools, grievance cells— basic needs....everything is provided for—but you have to ask; the government is bending backwards for rural welfare schemes. Unfortunately some villages as is yours are literally owned by the landlords. Fear of upsetting the great landlord binds them to adjust into whatever they have. The poor villagers are too scared to ask for more. The landlord thus is kept completely unaware of the dismal conditions his tillers are in. I guess Bindiya you have by some default become the spokesperson. You my dear with carry forth all the changes you need for your village!"

"Di-di...me speak to S-Shri Girdhariji...I can't...Bapu will never forgive me!"

"Bindiya, I can espouse your cause.....but I feel seeing you and hearing it from you will have a stronger effect. You have a very pure and convincing way of speaking! Don't worry Jeejaji is a wonderful human being. I am sorry Kamna didi behaved the way she did. I guess you really frightened her!"

Even if she wanted Bindiya could not suppress the bubble of laughter that threatened to burst forth.

Tanya caught her expression and soon the two were giggling

helplessly just thinking about how Kamna and Chaya had reacted to Bindiya's unexpected presence!

Thirteen

"My, my, you are very pretty under the grime!" Tany whistled lifting her glasses up and down on her nose, showing she was checking Bindiya out completely!

Bindiya embarrassedly glanced here and there not knowing how to accept the compliment.

Earlier, as soon as they had reached home Tanya passed instructions to Ammahji to help Bindiya bathe, "give her some clothes too!"

Ammahji driven by these instructions send off a 'driver bhaiya,' brother, running to the nearby market and to procure a cheap set of clothes. A suit, that comprised of one kurta, pyjama and chunnari, shirt, loose lowers, veil. Even though they were cheaply priced clothes, Bindiya loved them. They were no less than royal garments for her! Ammah-ji trying to be normal about washing up this bedraggled, at least in her mind, chit of girl, helped her bathe. Bindiya's frock was peeled off and she wrapped in a dressing gown! As for her frock.

"Aughhh! Smelly ….throw it away!" Bellowed Ammahji and the maids hurriedly complied.

Ammah-ji and two maids helped Bindiya shampoo and bathe.

Her ears, hands feet were given a thorough cleaning before they went behind the screen, which covered the bathing area of the bathroom, so Bindiya could bathe in privacy. Delicious scents from the soaps filled Bindiya's nostrils and she felt so clean. Ammah-ji taught her how to use the taps and soon over head artificial rain, shower, poured on her and she could not help giving an involuntary squeal. From behind the screen Ammah-ji instructed her to use the loofah and bath brushes to scrub properly. Her total ignorance about these cleaning agents had the maids and Ammah-ji in splits! Finally Bindiya got it right! When she was done, grumbling good humouredly Ammah-ji dried her hair with a thick fluffy towel, even as another white fluffy towel engulfed her. Fragrant oil was soaked into her hair and two pig tails affected. Ammahji quite taken up with these activities rubbed moisturizer into Bindiya's cheeks, hands and feet. She even squished her with perfume, "may as well go all the way in cleaning you up eh girl?" She chuckled!

Bindiya wore the new clothes. They fitted perfectly! Ammah-ji then guided her to Tanya and presented her with aplomb. Bindiya shyly accepted the compliments!

"Another good news, Bindiya, reports have come in saying Montu, Bontu, the others, will recover and be fine!"

Bindiya grinned widely, her happiness shinning bright from her eyes.

Even as Tanya was talking to Bindiya, Chaya strode in. Giving Bindiya a once-all over, she firmly turned her back and concentrated on picking up some comics lying by the bureau in the room. Tanya shrugged. Holding Bindiya by the elbow she led her out. "Bindiya, Jeejaji is in the 'baithak,' sitting room. I will come with you and take on when needed. But at first, you have to tell him everything."

Bindiya gulped—but did not protest as Tanya, opened the door and led her into a huge room.

Shri Girdhari was sitting on an arm chair. Next to him sat his wife Kamna. She was cracking betel nut and sprinkling betel leaves, paan, as she had been doing the other day. One servant stood around dutifully holding a tray.

The cold, chilling air hit Bindiya's face as soon as Tanya had opened the door that let them in."Shut the door, the AC is on." Tanya mumbled. "AC?" questioned Bindiya's mind but she didn't dwell further, since she was nervously assimilating her surroundings, and in an auto mode shut the door quickly!

Actually forgetting to wonder how the temperatures in the room were so cold. Bindiya had no idea about air conditioning obviously!

Blushing, Bindiya self consciously moved up to them.

"Jeejaji how many times have I told you too much of paan is not good for your health!" The smile on Tanya's face robbed the sting in the words.

"Ahh Tanu..." A bright smile spread over his chubby features, "Where have you been all day? Oh I see you have someone with you? Is it one of the scrap's you keep picking up from the streets eh?"

"Oh dear how you talk...no she is in fact one of your tiller's daughter."

"Really?   Who?"
"Deven."

"Aaaah...you came with your father the other day...er...you look different."

Kamna continued her task saying nothing but she glanced at Tanya with amusement.

"Yes, yes Jeejaji..*the* operative word is *difference*! She is here to talk to you about some differences you need to make!" Tanya said with some impatience.

"All right Girl. Talk to me." "Maalik commanded the quivering Bindiya.

Wide eyed and completely thrown by the state of affairs Bindiya tried to swallow, she failed miserably. Like a guppy fish she opened and closed her mouth.

Tanya came and held her shoulders, "please Bindiya *please*."

Taking charge of her wits, Bindiya steadied her nerves. Tanya's comforting hand gave her strength.

"Er....I...er Montu ...Jhumri died...." Bindiya began with a stammer.

Kamna rolled her eyes and sighed. For a moment Bindiya stalled her words seeing the action, but Shri Girdhari suddenly was interested. In a soft voice, he gently coaxed Bindiya to talk.

"Maalik...we ......" It was then Bindiya found the right words. Words flowed forth. She told him about the illness, the drain, the fear of him that suppressed the villagers. She told him of their dependence on Dayaji and disregard for medical help. Soon Shri Girdhari leant forward questioning her closely.

"Have you gone to school...you village children?" Girdhari asked.

"No Maalik...." Bindiya then told him about the back breaking chores they were doing.

When Bindiya finished Tanya added, "Jeejaji, I don't blame you... no one gets help till they ask for it. These people are poor, scared employed help...you have to uplift everything in that village. At least let my NGO help. We can set up camps and try and educate the villagers on hygiene etc. You need to pursue the authorities to built roads inside for them. I am sure this illness spreading can turn into an epidemic...we need to get health centres set up...... Tanya breathlessly added, "Mainly no vaccinations! There are suffering children in that settlement—all because they were not aware that a simple jab could help them!"

The company was silent in the wake of these words.

"What surprises me is they have been living like this forever, why has no one come to me yet?" Shr Girdhari thoughtfully commented.

"Jeejaji," Tanya replied as if talking to a child, "their way of living is not wrong. They live by the rules of nature literally! Only thing is they are unaware of the changing world that has brought pollution and degradation along with it. I admire these folks. They have value for everything they own and do. However, times have shrunk, *every possible way*, they can live the healthy, natural way they have been used to."

"Natural way? Is that not the best way?"

"I agree. *How I agree!* But we cannot forget that they too need progress in life. They are like people from a lost planet as far as you are concerned!"

Kamna raised her eyebrows not liking the way Tanya was speaking. But Shri Girdhari continued to listen.

"Look at these people: the hardy rural brand! They are tough… make a go of everything, no hardship bothers them, they invent and adjust!" Tanya breathlessly exclaimed, adding, "No lights? Take it from the pole, no vehicle? Make the 'jugaar' the list is endless!"

"So why do you want them to change?" Shri Girdhari leaned forward to ask.

"Jeejaji! *They have to adapt to the changed times.* Water has to be treated now, not like old days where the water table was high and water not silted thus prone to pollution, likewise the idea that if you live with it you become immune to it has to be erased. Flies and mosquitoes are now very dangerous as new strains of malaria, dysentery have evolved. Machines and smog have created another type of health concerns! They need to continue their life the way it is but add hygiene, awareness and education to it too!" She let her words sink in then she added, "I am not saying make shopping malls and high-tech pubs over here; just roads and links, to make their lives easier! Stay with the rural patterns, alongside enhance their lives with healthy options too!"

Bindiya gazed at Tanya. Her heart swelled with love for this lady who was taking up their cause.

"Did you see how they have catered for their own electricity? From a pole! Naked wires run through their village! Some authority gave them the electric pole then " Tanya shrugged in fly away action, Tanya paused, then excitedly continued, "they are like the forgotten people…. left on their own…. No one has come to check them out! How bad is that? Your friend that local politician.. he concentrates only on the vote heavy areas…not these small hardly populated villages….It is up to you to make the changes… Help them please…"

Kamna gazed up at the passion in her younger sister's tone. Bindiya's eyes darted to 'Maalik' judging his reactions to all this. She could discern nothing but only a concentrated curiosity at what Tanya was saying.

Tanya continued, "Jeejaji there is abundance here. Fruits, crops everything. Yet nothing to own or care for because of the fear of upsetting you! There has to be a balance. In their ignorance they are nurturing jaundice, dysentery, God knows what!" Tanya pushed back her glasses and passed an intense look to her audience, "But a free flying life is not all; why Jeejaji are their children not educated? Why don't we have schools here? Why no medical facilities…can't they own their own land……have better living facilities….don't they have a right to uplift and lead better lives? Or we leave them with open drains, fear for modern medicines, bonded and illiterate?"

There was an awkward silence.

Though Girdhariji did not answer he sighed and addressed Bindiya,

"I like your spirit er girl-no… what did you say her name is?"

"Bindiya" Kamna supplied actually turning to smile at Bindiya.

Bindiya blushed and stared at the mosaic floor.

"Bindiya…good spirit….of course I will help…bring Deven to me."

"No …'Saabji,' (boss man), you and I will visit the village!" Kamna firmly interrupted much to everyones surprise!

Bindiya whipped her head up and Tanya whistled!

Kamna was saying, "you know I think we need to go and help them…they are the ones who work and make all this," she waved at the house and grandeur, possible….Chaya needs to learn too."

Bindiya was smiling so hard her cheeks ached.

Tanya hugged her brother-in-law saying, "Jeejaji…get up we have to visit a sick child in the hospital!"

The news that Shri Girdhari was in the hospital asking for Deven spread like wild fire!

The hospital was owned by Shri Girdhari's family trust. The doctors and hospital management was naturally thrown into a tizzy. Not once in years had this happened. If Shri Girdhari or family needed medical help doctors went to the Haveli.

Nervously Deven jumped up when the great man and his entourage entered the corridor he was sitting in with Bontu and Shanta. Montu lay on a stretcher in the room in front. A glucose drip was attached to the back of his hand. Bontu had been medicated and was feeling much better. Chotu, Phuliya's mother and perhaps one or two more sick villagers were too somewhere in the hospital, getting treated!

"M-Maalik!" Deven stammered.

"Deven. I have come to see your son…both of them …how are they?"

"Er ..better Maalik y-your blessings…er!"

"Why did I not know you did not have roads, water, electricity, medical aid? Why did no one complain?" Shri Girdhari ji suddenly wanted to know from a startled Deven.

"Er …er…er" was all Deven could manage. He noticed that a crowd of spectators had build up around them.

"This girl…Bindiya your daughter is very brave…she had the guts……I hear you stopped her from coming to me?" Shri Girdhari beetled his eyebrows to ask.

Deven flushed and lowered his gaze. A loud guffaw broke the silence.

"Deven please I am not a monster. I just did not know…"

"Yes…we are just not aware…Bindiya came and told us and that is how we know that you people just lived with a certain condition and adapted yourselves around it; not asking for anything in fear of losing your jobs.. oh dear!" Kamna interrupted her husband. Her voice was kind and concerned. Deven felt his lips widen into a hesitant smile.

"Deven things are going to change from now on!"

These words rang forth with determined sincerity from Shri Girdhari!

Fourteen

SIX MONTHS LATER...

"Tanya didi if you plus two with five the answer is seven right?" Montu held up his slate to ask.

Tanya sitting on a chair smiled and gave a correct mark. She lifted her head and stared at the two rows of village children sitting on their mats. They all were neatly dressed in a blue shirt and blue pants for boys and blue skirt for girls. Their hair was washed and combed. No shoes for these students. They all wore rubber slippers. Tanya was amazed at how bright the children were. They took to learning swiftly!

"Wear clean neat clothes and always-always, wash your hands before meals!" Tanya droned again and again!

The children/villagers attentively began to follow the dictates of this young lady they were learning to love dearly.

She had immediately started rounding up help to get the children to school. An involuntary giggle escaped her. A bird swept down and perched on one of the children's head.

"Oieeee!" the kid self consciously brushed the bird away!

Tanya sighed, a deep rich sigh. These people were so simple. In-spite of all changes; the rural patterns remained; innocence of discovering a new way of life shining through brightly!

Bindiya too sat in the front row with her other brother Bontu. Tanya had decided to teach outdoors till the school building was completed.

A government grant to start a school had come in a month ago after the tireless efforts by Shri Girdhari. Shri Girdhari was using his power to move things fast!

Tanya did not want to wait. She applied to her NGO group to transfer her welfare project to this village, as well as the other villages needing help in these areas. As soon as she was granted permission she began to work here and all the other tiller settlements around, in her quest for improving conditions. It was like she had opened a can of worms! Disease, especially with the womenfolk was rampant; with only Daya-ji to depend on; keeping their complaints, mostly female problems, a secret they worsened the circumstances; and literally fostered ill health! With relief Tanya thought that is changing now!' Her awareness campaign's had effectively kicked off you see!

Tanya had innovatively opened the school under the banyan tree! Uniforms, chalks, slates and early learning books came from the help of her NGO.

This village as well as the neighbouring village was being given a total makeover. Sulabh, toilets, facilities, a health clinic and awareness camps were already in progress. The village drain had been covered and proposals to make their huts 'pucca,' solid, were under way. Plans for all these changes had been furnished to the local politician in power and welfare units by Shri Girdhari. All this would take time but everyone was ready to wait.

The biggest achievement was the central water tap installed in the village and the electricity situation addressed. With a lot of fanfare the local politician or MLA, Minister of legislative assembly, inaugurated the tap! With prodding from Girdhari electricity was restored properly too.

"I feel sad to know my farmlands had unlimited supply of electricity in the day time but my tillers had none by the evening!" Shri Girdhari would comment over and over.

Convincing the parents that their children needed time off from household chores to study was not a problem. Shri Girdhari made a visit to the village. His over awed company nodded dumbly when he commanded, "I have given land for the school building. I want your children in school from ten in the morning to two in the afternoon. Lunch will be given by me! Adults can attend evening school too. If we have the right numbers that can be started too.I mean school for the grownups!" Girdhari waited for the twitters at his comment to die before he added, "However, for the regular education for children, Tanya has proposed an outdoor school in the same complex till the building comes up. ...." He talked outlining future plans. Like a rainbow after a dark and unending storm, Bindiya emerged as quite the heroine. When Shri Girdhari began to visit the village more regularly, the tillers at first hesitantly then more confidently began to tell him their problems. "We have this girl to thank!" Shyam Taya patted Bindiya and announced sitting under the banyan tree one evening. Bindiya was thrilled as pride reflected from both her parents faces.

What was really good was that Shanta got an opportunity to show her ankle to a doctor. Though surgery was ruled out; medicines and some exercises eased her pain considerably! Every time the doctor saw Shanta, she marvelled at how Shanta had survived the hackneyed, stitching job done by Dayaji, without infection! More stories of how the benefit of going to a doctor emerged and somehow it seemed the *entire village had some secret health problem or the other!*

Even a dentist with his team visited the villages once a month, managed through the offices of the NGO. He came to give them knowledge on oral health! "Neem sticks are the best. But along with that teeth needs to be cleaned. Now this is how you use a tooth brush and paste!" Said the dentist when he discovered that at least 30% of the villagers suffered from tooth decay due to carelessness and were dependant on only neem sticks for cleansing!

Dayaji realised that his art of ancient medicine could be enhanced with knowledge of regular medicines too. He began to undertake only cases he thought he could safely care for. After all natural healing is also a good option. However, most of the time Dayaji advised, "You need blood tests, urine samples and a thorough check up. Go to the hospital!"

Suddenly hospital was not a bad place. The villagers learnt that their women folks would be cared by lady doctors in respect to their age old fear of male doctors. Montu and Bontu as well as the rest being completely restored to health, lent credibility that hospitals cured! Slowly this awareness was taking a positive shape.

Presently, Tanya looked down at the papers on her lap. She picked out a letter and read its contents. Then smiling brightly she cleared her throat and announced,

"I have news for you. Bindiya please stand up." Bindiya shyly stood up.

"Bindiya for your bravery in bringing to our notice the changes this village needed you are going to be given an award!"

The children began to clap. Bindiya licked her lips and bashfully looked here and there.

"You are happy nah?"

Bindiya inaudibly nodded. Suddenly her mind remembered how Shri Girdhari had praised her and her father had accepted that Bindiya had been very brave! Shanta and her brothers were so proud of her too!

"Bindiya on independence day you will be awarded a prize by Shri...,she took the local politicians name. A rousing round of claps drowned her voice when it died down, then only a singular clap could be heard. It was Kamna.

Her presence made everyone sit up. Bindiya too straightened.

Kamna had begun to teach the children too. Chaya had left for her school abroad. Chaya had quite changed before leaving and she looked forward to her next vacations so she could help her mother and aunt with all these emerging changes!.

Kamna smiled and pulled up the other plastic chair and sat with her sister.

Suddenly a voice broke through! "Lazy girls walk faster….."

Ammah-ji unaware that she could be heard was shouting, "Don't be slack, go, go fast."

Escorting her were two guards carrying big tiffin carrier's of food. Two maids followed behind too. Every day, Kamna provided a mid-day meal for the children. Every day Ammah-ji arrived with this entourage!

When Ammah-ji came into view and reached them, a burst of laughter greeted her. Her shouting instructions comically silenced on seeing Kamna and Tanya, and the children laughed louder. Ammah-ji stopped in confusion wondering why everyone was laughing. Kamna gave the children a "don't tease her look" and asked Ammah-ji to quickly lay the food.

Bindiya sat down and hugged her knees. She absorbed her happiness within. Her glance caught her scrubbed clean feet and hands, she reached up to touch her washed and combed hair. Her mind roamed to all the good things happening around her. She gave a deep sigh and thought,

"Hmmmm, Tanya didi told us which soaps to use and how to clean ourselves… how to live in a better environment….. everything is changing for the good……..I am so, so, so happy. Yes…so, so *happy I rebelled!*"

THE END